Where the Fishermen Sing

a novel

by Anna Careless

Creative Bound Inc.
P.O. Box 424, Carp, Ontario
Canada K0A 1L0

ISBN 0-921165-21-8
Printed and bound in Canada

Art Direction: Wendelina O'Keefe
Cover Design & Illustration: Michaela Ford

Canadian Cataloguing in Publication Data

Careless, Anna
Where the fishermen sing

ISBN 0-921165-21-8

1. Title.

PS8555.A7312W43 1992 C813'.54 C92-090274-X
PR9199.3.C37W43 1992

To my husband, Richard

and to

Janet Adams

Part
1

1

Canso, Nova Scotia, 1935

Laurie looked out at the sea from the cabin of the *Owera* with large apprehensive eyes. Suddenly the boat felt too small in a sea so large and violent. The waves like gigantic curling tongues rose up as if trying to reach out and suck them into the depths of the ocean. When a towering wall of water came rolling toward her, she buried her face in Grandma Lila's wool coat. She remained like this, clinging to her for reassurance, her heart drumming in her ears, until the wave slammed over the boat. Looking up, she held her breath; she could see nothing but water. For a moment she thought they must be sinking, until the *Owera* lurched up, once again discarding its burden of sea, and Laurie gasped for air.

"It looks far worse that it is," Lila said. "I've made this crossing since I was a child and we always get home safe and sound. Perhaps it would be better, my dear, if you don't look."

When Laurie realized that the *Owera* could be completely covered with water without sinking, she felt an awe and an excitement, the same feeling that she had when watching a violent thunderstorm. She stayed by the window of the cabin so as not to miss that which she feared, because, after all, was this not an adventure?

Once the *Owera* reached the shelter of some islands, the sea, though choppy, became kinder. The passengers who had been too ill to stand slowly recovered and made weak attempts to freshen up. The red of Laurie's coat stood out against their dark clothing, attracting attention. When a roly-poly man with a droopy handlebar moustache smiled at her, she smiled back shyly, trying not to stare. Laurie didn't like it when people looked at her for long. It made her feel uncomfortable.

It was in the evening just before sunset, under a pink sky, when the *Owera* docked in Canso harbour. The anchor chain rumbled into place as Lila sighed, "home at last." Just a few feet from shore, directly in front of them, was the back of her house.

"It's so big," Laurie said. They disembarked single file and made their way up the narrow path and through the back garden towards the front of the house on Main Street.

"The ground feels funny," Laurie said as she struggled with her small bag.

Grandma laughed. "We still have our sea legs," she said.

They reached the home that, until that moment, Laurie had only seen in a snapshot. The delicate white latticework trim reminded Laurie of the lacy edging inside a box of chocolates and the fancy turret on the roof made her think of Fairyland castles.

Once inside, they climbed a gracious staircase onto a landing, and from there entered on the left, into the largest bedroom Laurie had ever seen.

"Where's my room, Grandma?" she said.

"You'll be here with me," Lila pointed to a cot in the corner. "It will be nice to have company," ...and then because Laurie's face expressed such disappointment, she added, "It can get pretty damp and cold on some evenings, even in the summer; I can only heat a few bedrooms. The others are sealed off."

"How many are there, Grandma?"

"Six in all, three across the hall on the next landing."

The master bedroom led into a small parlour and, to the right, they stepped down into a narrow kitchen with a massive wood stove. At the far end of the room, a narrow staircase led downstairs.

While Lila kindled a fire to take the dampness out of things, Laurie explored further. Off the kitchen, a dark corridor accessed two tiny maids' rooms and a large bathroom. The furniture was old and faded but it still retained its Victorian elegance. Having come from a small modern apartment, Laurie felt that she had entered into a different time, as in a play or film.

The little kitchen was once a laundry room where the maids washed and boiled the clothes, the back stairs busy with their comings and goings. "Our maids were Irish," Lila said. "Once I found Maureen, who came in on washdays, saying her beads in the linen closet. 'It's good to pray, Maureen,' I said, 'but first you must finish the washing.' " Lila thought it was a funny story and laughed, but Laurie thought some disaster might have occurred that needed prayers right away.

Lila also told her about Grandpa Moffatt who had died a few years earlier. He was part owner of the Whitman store with his partner, Mr Rice. Laurie had only a vague recollection of him, as she was only three when she had last visited Canso with her father. She remembered that he was tall, had a moustache, and used a cane. "Why was the store called Whitman's instead of Moffatt's, Grandma?"

"That was a courtesy because Mr Whitman owned it first."

As she listened to her grandmother, Laurie could easily visualize the house full of laughing children, Hazel, Donald, Harding and Jamie her dad. She fell asleep that night while picturing Grandma managing the servants and cooking delights for Grandpa, who reigned over all in the Victorian manner.

Laurie was still sleeping soundly before sunrise, when the small Norwegian fishing fleet left harbour. When the sailing vessels returned, heavy with the morning catch of fish, she was lying awake listening to the sounds of morning. Grandma was making porridge in the kitchen, somewhere downstairs a screen door slammed. Outside on the wharf a sailor gave a signal to his mates. Then something extraordinary happened.

The fishermen began to sing in chorus as they hauled in their nets; the Norwegian love song, sad and filled with longing, mingled with the piping of gulls and the whispering water and was carried on a gentle breeze into her room. Laurie gasped with delight and ran to the window. Below her the sun spangled the bay, white sails bobbed and gulls dove about the wharf. Farther off, a red-capped lighthouse perched on the end of a small island. Laurie leaned out of the window as far as she could as if to embrace the sun-washed scene before her. She would never see or hear anything more wondrous, not if she lived to be a hundred.

From that day onward, she would spend many an hour up on the cliffs watching the waves crash against the rocks and rush out to sea, then crash again, till drawing closer she felt the gentle spume upon her face, anointing her, forever a child of the sea.

The next day she was given a tour of the ground floor: a kitchen big enough to roller skate in, a large elegant dining room with a mantled hearth, and a parlour with another hearth. A conservatory which housed a piano had folding doors that opened into yet another room. This lower floor was rented to a couple who had a daughter a few years older than Laurie.

"It seemed the sensible thing to do," Grandma said, "as I can use the extra income to maintain the place." She had been shocked to find that she was left with very meagre financial resources after her husband died, the store having been mortgaged.

There was one bedroom upstairs Grandma forbade Laurie to enter "because," she said, "Grandpa died there." Since Laurie knew very little about death, she wondered if someone or something might still be in there.

Grandma Lila often talked to Laurie like this, as if she were talking to an adult, taking it for granted that the girl knew what she meant. She said that the tasselled ropes in the rooms upstairs were to fetch the maids. Laurie wondered how pulling on a rope could get a maid, unless the rope was tied to her waist at the other end, which of course was silly.

Laurie's first outing was to visit her grandmother's brother and his wife, Uncle Will and Aunt Lena Bigelow who lived across the street. Their spacious Victorian home was a landmark, being the town hotel; it was also home to Great-Grandma "Muzzie" Bigelow.

Grandma sailed into the kitchen with Laurie in tow and introduced her. Aunt Lena remarked on Laurie's long braids, Uncle Will smiled and winked in lieu of conversation. Then a tapping sound came from the ceiling. Laurie looked up. "That's Muzzie," Lila said. "Why don't you bring up her tea and surprise her."

Laurie had never seen her great-grandmother and her first impression was one of shock. She didn't want to remain long in that room on her first meeting, as she felt uneasy.

Muzzie's appearance was startling. She was tiny and

frail, her face a mask of wrinkles, and hanging nearly to the floor was a thick white braid of hair. Her eyes, a pale watery blue, seemed to bore right through Laurie as if to read her thoughts. Her nightgown was long, white, beribboned and flowing. Laurie thought she had a "half way to heaven" look about her, rather like an ancient angel, if indeed there was such a thing, and she would not have been surprised at all if Muzzie had suddenly floated up and out of the window.

Then the question came; it would always be the same question. "Tell me, dearie, how many places are there for people who die?" A Catholic by upbringing, Laurie was obliged to say three places, Heaven, Purgatory and Hell, knowing all the while that Muzzie knew of only two places, being a Baptist.

Laurie's teacher back home said that Protestants, Jews and pagans went to Heaven the same as Catholics did because they didn't know any better. The girl had no wish to be impolite, so she took Muzzie's corrections meekly. After all, she was older than old, and Laurie sensed that she didn't have long to live.

The truth was that Muzzie secretly relished the idea of a place in between as she had been quite avant-garde in her day.

Laurie could tell that the old woman loved her, however, by the way she looked at her with her bright, teary eyes and called her "Jamie's little girl." She had a soft spot for Laurie's father and told her stories about him.

Until this time, Laurie only thought of Jamie as her father, but before long she was able to see him as a boy and a young man. He was always losing his mittens and hats, went around town looking thrown together. "He didn't give a hoot," Muzzie said.

The story that most impressed Laurie was the one about heartbreak. Muzzie smiled impishly as she said, "Your dad had a girlfriend named Gladys who threw him over. He was so upset that he tore down a row of fences on main street. He was the talk of the town for months." Laurie had seen her dad angry, so she could well imagine the incident. She begged for more stories, and would hear some every time she visited.

Laurie also loved to pore over the old photographs, some made of tin. Muzzie gave her great grand-daughter a feeling for history and in a sense, Laurie gave the old woman something more to live for. "You, Laurie, will be the keeper of the flame," Muzzie said.

It was the beginning of July when Laurie, looking down from her window, saw the boy. He was inspecting a vegetable garden, hands in his pockets, facing away from her. What struck her was the way the sun flickered on his blond hair and shot little sparks into her eyes.

"Grandma, who's the boy in the garden?"

"That must be Tommy Doyle. He stays downstairs with my tenants every summer."

Then he turned and when Laurie saw his face, her heart gave a lurch. "Oh Grandma, he's *so* handsome."

Grandma laughed and thought this amusing, but she proved to be an ally in this game of love, introducing them at the next opportunity.

Laurie didn't say much on that first meeting because she was too immersed in feelings. She was smitten! To her dismay, he was twelve years *old* and she would only be nine in September. She knew boys of that age, even her brother Murdo, liked girls to be older because all they thought about was breasts.

Until she met Tommy, Laurie was not overly concerned about her appearance. Looking in the mirror, she tried to see herself through his eyes: tall for her age and inclined to be very thin, with as yet no hint of breasts, her hair done up in two long braids. Adults said she had lovely eyes. They pulled her braids playfully and said, "Look at what you have, aren't you lucky!" They called them plaits. Pigs' tails! that's what they are, she thought, and proceeded to unravel them.

Combing her hair loose, she tucked it behind her ears and put a dab of Grandma's lipstick on. Her lips were on the thin side, but her face did look softer and rather pretty with loose hair. She began to carry a small comb in her pocket and vowed that the next time Tommy was around, this is what he would see. When she knew he was coming she frantically undid her braids, combed her hair, and posed in what she thought to be a very romantic position on the swing. Laurie had only two dresses, the one with polka dots which she loved and the wine with pink inserts which she hated. For Tom, she wore whichever was clean.

Now Tom not only looked at her differently, but stopped to ask what grade she was in and then to engage her in conversation. At first he couldn't figure out what it was about her that was different except for the loose hair, then realized it was her eyes. In what way they were so different he couldn't have said; he only knew that they were beautiful and that if he looked at them, he felt like he did right after confession, like he was walking on air.

Laurie lived for these moments, however brief. But the course of love did not run smoothly, for she was told that Tommy had a girlfriend.

Laurie's first impression on seeing her was that she looked grown up. Her face would have been pretty if it were not for a lot of pimples. Laurie felt lucky, for her own skin was perfect. When she heard the girl speak, however, heard how soft and gentle her voice was, she understood why Tommy liked her.

But all the girls loved Tommy and it was easy to see why. His smile was just crooked enough to make him irresistible, and when he laughed his eyes sparkled, so that she remembered them for a while after he was gone, and then she would laugh too. They were the nicest blue Laurie had ever seen, not pale but a deep blue. She liked the way he walked, with his hands in his pockets. He wore knee socks with short pants; she couldn't help looking at his legs, especially his knees. Though she didn't understand why at the time, it was the *maleness* in him that stirred her.

Having never before felt this pleasant, if unsettling, agitation, she assumed that she must be in love, and so enjoyed it the only way she knew how, namely, to be wherever he was. To her delight, she discovered that he was a Catholic, and consequently, one of the places she was sure to see him was at Mass.

Since Lila was a Baptist, Laurie went to church with her on Sunday evening, but she also attended Mass in the morning. She knew her teacher and the priest back home wouldn't like the idea of her going to a Protestant church. At first she worried about it, but when she discovered that the service consisted of hymns, a few prayers and a small sermon, she couldn't understand what all the fuss was about. The hymns and prayers were about God and Jesus and they even said the Our Father, adding an extra line on the end about the power and the glory, a part so stirring to Laurie that she adopted it, but surreptitiously, lest someone tell her she was doing wrong.

But a Baptist church service was vastly different from the Catholic Mass which was said in Latin. Grandma said, "*Our* service is in English so that everyone can understand."

This was a double-meaning remark, which Laurie recognized immediately. She pointed out to Lila that she understood the Mass and proceeded to say the Our Father and Hail Mary in Latin. Lila was very impressed, so when anyone came to visit, Laurie was asked to give a repeat performance.

Nevertheless, she did wonder about the difference between a Minister and a Priest. A minister could marry and somehow that made him less holy in her eyes, but when she first heard him give a sermon she was fascinated, not because of what he was saying but because of how he said it. Up and down the words went in such a strange way that it was almost like praying. She decided that a minister was holy too because he sounded like God must have sounded when he gave the Ten Commandments to Moses.

Even so, going to church twice on Sunday would have been tedious, except for the fact that Tommy was there. While the priest droned on with his sermon, she could look at Tommy and transport herself into another dimension.

It happened one day that they left the church together and walked home by way of the cliffs around the bay. The wharf was quiet, the sound of gulls crooning above the surf. An occasional popcorn cloud sailed across the sky. It was a perfect day, that Laurie was to remember always.

"Some day I'll go to sea," Tom said.

"Oh how exciting, how I wish that girls could be sailors! I love to read sea stories. Did you read *The Little Mermaid*?"

"No, but I read *Treasure Island* and *Kidnapped.* I'll lend them to you if you like, that is if you're able to read them."

"Tommy Doyle, I bet I can read anything you can."

As they strolled along the beach, Tom showed her shells, knowing each by name. Laurie was extremely curious and he happily answered all of her questions, eager to show her how much he knew. The hours flew by; Laurie wished she could stay longer. "Grandma's waiting and I'm already late," she said.

Tom was wearing his Sunday suit and as he stood there, pale blond and clean, against a background of dark cliff, Laurie thought he was the handsomest boy she had ever seen. Tom met her eyes and gulped. "So long," he said, and pretended to be busy.

When Laurie shut the door a feeling of desolation swept over her, for she realized that one day she would leave Canso and Tommy, most probably forever. After those few hours on the beach, there occurred a subtle change in their relationship. At first Tom allowed her to tag along on his hunt for shells, thinking it a kindness on his part, but once Laurie had her foot in the door, she set about making herself very useful. Not only did she have a quick eye for spotting, but she had a genuine interest in the task at hand. She considered seashells to be truly beautiful gifts from the sea that could be made into a necklace or a bracelet. Though her interest was more in their ornamental value, she revered Tom for his knowledge and began under his tutelage to refer to the shells by name. Although she didn't realize it, she made Tom feel very important. She considered him to be an expert and his collection to be of great significance. Till now his rows of catalogued shells were regarded as a childish, albeit a wholesome, hobby. No one showed much interest in them, possibly because they were a common occurrence thereabouts, but Laurie was different.

When she said with compete candour, "Some day when you're finished, your collection will be in a museum and you will be famous," he not only considered his endeavours in a new perspective, but saw Laurie in a new light.

One day he showed her a wooden box in which he catalogued his shells. It was expertly made with different-sized compartments and a glass lid for viewing. "Where did you get it?" she asked.

"My Dad made it for me. He was a ship's carpenter."

"Where is your Dad now?"

"He died two years ago in a shipwreck near Sable Island."

She felt stunned and tried to think of something appropriate to say. "It's a perfect box," was all that she managed, and then, "Are you still very sad?"

"I am when I think about him but I don't think of him all the time like I did at first so I guess it's better. But Mom still cries a lot. She has to work now and that's why I'm staying with my aunt as much as possible. We live in Halifax; I go home for a weekend sometimes."

"Do you have a grandmother?"

"She lives in Ireland. You're lucky. You have two brothers and a sister, and all those relatives."

"And you're my best friend. Am I *your* best friend, Tommy?"

"You're my girl friend but don't tell anybody."

Laurie felt so happy that she wanted to tell the whole world, but instead she went around grinning to herself and looking a bit soft in the head.

It was around this time that Laurie met Captain Simms. He was a permanent fixture on the wharf, and everybody knew him. He had bushy white hair and an even bushier white beard that set him apart from other men. But it was the twinkle in his eyes that drew her, or rather the twinkle in one eye, as most of the time he was squinting. His face was a mass of brown leathery looking grooves from which a pipe jutted more often than not; his hands, brown and knotted like an old tree, were always busy at something: whittling, tying knots or cleaning fish. Though he was old, he did not seem so, being strong and full of vigour.

He knew where the fish were, better than any other, sensed when a squall was due before the others got wind of it, and he was respected for his advice which was generally very sound. He kept a small craft by the wharf which he pampered. Laurie thought it very pretty and inviting. She wanted to go to the little island to see inside the lighthouse and saw the captain as a means of getting there.

Shyly, she approached him one day, pretending to be interested in the fish he had caught. She watched him silently, hoping he would speak to her, but he seemed unaware of her presence. Just when she was about to give up and leave, he said casually, as if they had already been engrossed in conversation all along, “Yep, a storm be brewin’, a big ‘un. Best pack up an’ batten down.”

Then he looked at her with his squinty eye and said, “Ken ye ‘ear them singin’?” She looked around, for she could hear no singing and then she said, “Who do you hear?”

“Why, the mermaids, girlie, the mermaids.”

He beckoned her closer with a conspiratorial air. Laurie laughed and stepped forward. She was prepared to go along with the fantasy but the captain would have none of it.

“Ye scoff but after ye’ve been ‘ere a long while ye’ll no scoff, fer to be sure when the waves git real swarmy they carry the sound. There were times too, when I’ve ‘eard them, so loverly was their singin’ that I’ve ‘ad te plug me ears so’s te stay myself from diving in after them like a raving lunitic.”

He looked so wise and spoke with such certainty that she believed he had indeed heard something, and wondered if it could be true.

Fascinated by his manner of speaking and enthralled by the very idea of mermaids, she wanted to hear more. Now nothing could keep her away from the old man.

He not only took her to Hart’s Island and showed her the lighthouse, but he took her to several others too. The one he found most interesting though, was called Grassy Island. “Aye there’s ‘istory here,” he said, and showed her the remains of a fort.

But it was Durrell's Island that captured Laurie's imagination, for it was a summer camping ground for the micmac. The captain was well liked by the Indians, so Laurie spent several hours among them. She watched a group of women making baskets to be sold on the mainland, and because they had such open smiling faces, was soon talking to them. When she left, they referred to her as "the one who never stops asking questions."

The captain answered some of them, teaching her all he knew about the history of the islands, but more than a tour guide he was an entertainer. Laurie loved his singing. She quickly adapted to his lingo and listened to sea shanties, some funny, some sad, but the ones she loved best were wondrously mysterious, telling of life beneath the sea where another kingdom existed, eerie and beautiful, the home of the mermaids.

But Laurie gave something to the captain as well. Little did she know that she had come at a time when he needed her. His life's mate had died that year and he was sore of heart. Laurie recounted the story of *The Little Mermaid* by Hans Christian Andersen which he had never heard, and she recited all the poems which she had learned in school, with feeling. He was moved by her enthusiasm for life and wondered at how deep a thinker she was for someone so young. She asked so many questions and sometimes helped him answer them. Yet at times she was so quiet that they shared the same thoughts, those born of the sea, the tranquillity, the very moods of the bay. She gave him little time for mourning, and so he healed. He would miss her when she was gone.

"Cap," she said, "I wish I had an island all of my own. If I was rich, I would buy an island and live on it, and oh, how I wish that my dad would move us all to Canso!, for I will miss it so. How could he leave a place so perfect?"

"Aye girlie, there's them that leave, but their 'eart calls em back. He'll feel the call o' the sea an' go to it if he can, and if he cannot he'll na be an 'appy man."

On their last day together the bay was uncommonly calm and so he took her far out near the tip of the cape. There were no gulls mewing, no waves rolling, just a slap against the hull, and a gentle breeze, so gentle, like feathers on their cheeks warmed by the sun.

"Cap," said Laurie, "why did they call the town Canso? Surely they could have thought of a better name. Uncle Don said that the name started from an argument. He said that two men built a boat house, but when they built the boat, one of the men said it could not fit in the boat house. The other said, 'it can so.' They argued, 'can so' and 'can not,' but the boat did fit in, so they named the place Canso. Is that true Cap, or was Uncle Donald teasing me again?"

Cap shook with laughte. "Yer Uncle Don's a card 'ee is. Nay Laurie, t'is na true, for Canso is from the Micmac, the first C'nadians who lived here b'for us all. They were first ter name the places and they called them as they sawr them, direct like. T'was called Kamsok, meaning opposite the lofty cliffs."

"Oh Cap, how exciting, an Indian name! I'm so glad I met you, you know just about everything."

Just then Cap felt a monstrous tugging on his line; a battle ensued between man and fish that promised a prize catch. Laurie stared at the water with anticipation, thinking that it must be a shark or a whale that made the line bend like that. She feared the captain would be pulled into the water. Finally, with the aid of a net, the catch was brought in flapping its defiance about their feet, a giant halibut.

Laurie had never seen a fish so big and so pretty. Its scales looked like glistening sequins as the sun played upon them. The fish was so active that it leapt up and slammed back on her feet, its mouth opening and closing, its one visible eye seeming to implore her to do something.

"Oh Cap, please put it back," Laurie cried, "it's so beautiful!"

The captain thought to comfort her. "T'is the way o' the sea, girlie. She can fill a lott'er stumuchs." But Laurie would not be comforted.

Because she was so upset, down on the deck, stroking the back of the fish, crooning, and because she would be leaving soon, the captain did something that he had thought he never would do. He heaved the fish overboard, clamped his head in his hands and said, "I've gone daft for sure!"

Laurie ran to the rail shouting, "thank you Cap, thank you!" The fish flipped over, righted itself, and took one gigantic leap into the air before it skimmed off into the deep.

The captain shook his head in bewilderment and then stared out to sea. Laurie sensed that because of her, he had lost something valuable, so she kept quiet, looking not at him but out across the water with a dazed look. They remained so for a while not speaking, and when Laurie suddenly said to him in a voice full of wonder, "I can hear them! I can really hear them! The mermaids are singing!" He wiped a tear from his eye.

The next day, Laurie's uncle Donald came home on furlough from the army. Because of this unexpected event, Grandma was unable to accompany her back home in time for school opening, and so Laurie was to commence her schooling in Canso. It turned out to be an experience she would not have wanted to miss.

The complete informality of this school in a poor country town was a vivid contrast to the Catholic girls' academy back home in St Laurent. The teacher, who was pretty and pleasantly plump, was Don's sweetheart, Brenda Rice.

Don always made Laurie giggle and always had a story to tell. Once, at dinner, after he had come from visiting Brenda, he said, "Brenda sat on her oven door while we were talking and eating muffins. She was so fat, the door broke off and she landed on the floor." Laurie visualized the episode all too clearly and laughed so much that she had a coughing fit.

Donald had red curly hair and talked in a staccato. She couldn't help but like him and she soon found out that everybody did.

But as far as school went, there was no Catechism and no tension whatsoever. Laurie was at least two years ahead of the others in reading ability and though she had a problem with Math, it was nothing that could not be remedied. Brenda gave her sums to do when she came to Grandma's once a week for a sewing bee, and Laurie soon caught up.

Although she couldn't relate to the sewing bees because the talk was about people she didn't know, and though she had to do sums for nearly two hours, the evening wasn't a complete loss. It was her job to pass around the dainty sandwiches and cakes. They were scrumptious and she had permission to eat anything left on the table.

When the ladies finished sipping their tea and dabbed their lips with embroidered napkins, Grandma played the piano. Laurie loved to listen to the melodies. "I'll take you home again Kathleen," they sang, and she wondered why Kathleen wasn't at home. Her favourite was "The Old Rugged Cross." At times like this, she was proud of her grandmother; all eyes were upon her.

Lila Moffatt had class. Comparatively tall for a woman of her era, she held her head high. She sat straight in her chair and had a horror of getting what she called "round shouldered." She had a lovely face, having been blessed with a straight proportionate nose, perfect skin and wide-set eyes of a delicate bluish grey. Particular about her appearance, she dressed in a very elegant fashion, placing a special emphasis on her hats. Sometimes as she sat before her mirror, she would ask Laurie to help her choose one. The "putting on of the hat" was the final touch, a ritual unto itself. Tilting it this way and that until the perfect angle presented itself, Lila then secured it with a large pin.

To Grandmother *appearances* were of the utmost importance. One day at dinner, Lila told Don that Mrs Smith had hung her wash at the side of the house in full view of the street. She then laughed and made a patronizing remark about "such people," adding "What can you expect?"

Don became annoyed, "They're just as good as we are," he said, whereupon his mother bristled with indignation.

Her face flushed a deep pink as she replied, "Donald! how can you *say* such a thing?" Don looked at Laurie, laughed and then meowed and hissed, pretending that a cat was under the table.

But unless one jumped to conclusions about Lila Moffatt, she was not as it would seem on first impression, because no honest work was beneath her. If the necessity arose, she would do it. This Laurie saw first hand, when to her horror she found out that the toilets didn't flush. Her grandmother explained that in the past, the servants had emptied them, but now she did it. Laurie watched her row out to the middle of the bay and accomplish the distasteful task. She also chopped wood for the big stove, dug in the garden, scrubbed floors, and did whatever, as she said, "had to be done." She also nursed her husband Harding for several years till his death after he was bedridden with a stroke, a labour not only of love, but of duty — in itself a very noble act.

Yet when one met her for the first time and saw her

dressed elegantly, most likely playing the piano, one would never guess that she could, as Rudyard Kipling so aptly put it, "walk with kings nor lose the common touch."

Although Laurie was beginning to feel a bit anxious about getting home, having been absent an uncommonly long time, she was by no means unhappy. She was always making discoveries; adventure followed her.

Tom took her down to the edge of town to see a strong man pull a truck with his teeth but when he passed his hat around she didn't have anything to put in it, which was embarrassing. It just wasn't fair, she thought, that a brave and strong man was so poor. He never got more than a dollar change in his hat; she hoped that in the winter he would do better.

"When it's really cold," Tom said, "he will sit on a block of ice in his bathing suit and eat an ice cream cone."

Sometimes she would go to the grocery store down by the wharf, where Mr Rice, the owner, would weigh her on the giant meat scales. It was Mr Rice who told her about the widow's walk on top of Grandma's roof and the larger one on the Whitman house next door. He lowered his voice to a near whisper as he pointed them out to her and said, " Wives and sweethearts would scan the sea from there, for a sight of the ship that would bring their loved one home again; sometimes they never came back."

The very idea of a widow's walk inflamed Laurie's imagination, and so at the next opportunity, she found the place. Suspecting that Grandma would consider it dangerous, she wisely kept quiet.

Sometimes she would sneak up the rickety stairs and, from her vantage point, become so entranced with the romance and tragedy that overcame her imagination that she became a fair maiden waiting in vain for her sweetheart. It was there that she suddenly understood the meaning of Tennyson's poem that she had learned by rote in school.

Break, Break, Break, at the foot of thy crags o sea!
But the tender Grace of a day that is dead
Will never come back to me.

She recited the poem and for just a few moments would feel the pain as if her own. But she wasn't often in the mood for the widow's walk, because it was a sad place.

Another sad place was Johnny Sloan's house. He was the boy who sat next to her in school. He had bare feet. Laurie had never before seen anyone in school with bare feet. She listened enthralled as he told her stories of bravado, in which he was always the hero, and in which he always walked barefoot in the freezing winter snows, with no adverse effect on his person. She believed some of the stories, for it was September and he didn't seem to feel the cold even when it rained. She overflowed with pity to think that such a brave person should not walk in shoed dignity! But the visit made her feel uncomfortable; she became conscious of her own shoes till they became a guilty weight upon her feet.

One of her favourite haunts was Uncle Will's hotel. It was there, in the dining room, she loved to don an oversized white apron and serve table as her aunt and uncle dished out the delicious home-cooked meals. She pretended to be a waitress, and at that particular time no position was more meaningful to her. The clientele were mostly Norwegian fishermen. She couldn't understand their language but they always had a smile or a compliment for her, and a compliment she understood in any language. Like all little girls, she loved flattery.

There occurred, however, an embarrassing incident that tinged her career as a waitress. On leaving the dining room one of the fishermen dropped some money down the front of her dress and laughingly pinched her cheek. He thought of his own daughter whom he missed. Laurie ran into the kitchen and displayed her treasure, forty-five cents! Thrilled to think that for the first time in her life she had some pocket money, in no time flat she bought two pennies' worth of licorice and gum drops.

There was something else she had to do. She ran all the way to the edge of town. The strong man wasn't there but his truck was, and perched on the fender was his red hat. Laurie put ten cents in it. After all, she had seen him put the rope between his teeth and pull that truck three times.

She skipped home with a light heart, only to be told she must return the money as it was meant as payment for the meal, not as a gratuity. Sheepishly, she returned to the hotel and in a state of acute embarrassment, placed her ill-gotten treasure on the table minus twelve cents. Lena and Will watched in silence. Though they said not a word, she knew somehow that they shared her discomfort. They would have liked to have given her the money, but hard times would not permit it.

If the truth were known, it was Laurie's uncle Will Bigelow who, years ago, had run a small bootlegging operation from her grandmother's cellar. The potatoes for the Whitman store were stored down there. Lila couldn't figure out why her brother spent so much time in the cellar with the potatoes. Laurie's grandfather Harding Moffatt was, among other things, the town Magistrate, so Will thought it was the perfect place to hide the liquor. He assumed that nobody would ever think to check there. He was mistaken, but that is another story. At that time the telegraph office was in Uncle Will's hotel, definitely not a safe place for his undercover operations.

"Aunt Lena and Uncle Will Bigelow said they were

going to sell the hotel and move to Montreal," Laurie said. "Why would anyone who lived in Canso want to go to Montreal?"

"Because of the Depression, dear," Grandma said. Laurie didn't really understand, thinking it meant that nearly everyone was depressed about not having enough money to buy things. She guessed it was why Uncle Will never gave her the promised nickel, even when she scratched his back for a whole five minutes. But she never had meals better than what they gave her and the memory of their hot pies she would almost taste. She would smile when she thought of her uncle Will juggling a piece of hot blueberry pie around in his mouth as he said, "Thish pie ish shoh hot, I feelsh ash if I'm in hell."

The fateful day came when Laurie went downstairs to say goodbye to Tommy. He offered her a book and said, "I bet that you can't read this." Laurie knew that she could read anything he gave her and read she did. He was really surprised and Laurie glowed. Tom looked around to see if he was observed, then he quickly gave Laurie a kiss on the cheek. Reaching out, he offered her a shell. "It's a special one, there aren't many of them." He told her its name which she didn't hear because of the rushing in her ears, but if it had been a precious gem, she could not have been happier.

She wanted to give him something appropriate in return and racked her brain for an idea as she twiddled with the medal around her neck. "I know! You can have my St Christopher medal to protect you when you go to sea. He is the patron of travellers." She lifted it from her head and placed it around his neck.

It was then that he noticed the tag on her coat with her name and address on it. Laurie had meant to hide it but forgot. He said, "Why are you tagged?" She was to return to

Montreal with her aunt Lena. Although she was certainly old enough to travel without a tag, Grandma insisted on one, just in case the two got separated. Only babies wear tags, she thought. He must think I'm a baby!

Luckily, she didn't have to explain because a bell tinkled near the wall; she finally understood how the tasselled ropes worked. Grandma's voice came from a tube in the wall near the bell. She said it was time to go. Laurie was really impressed and remained so. It was a very good system of peaceful communication, she thought, far better than yelling up and down stairs.

So Laurie said goodbye with her heart in her eyes, the shell clutched tightly in her hand. She was to remember Tommy often over the years. She thought he was lost to her forever, but in this she was mistaken.

Where the Fishermen Sing

Below the cliffs of Canso
The breakers lash their spray
If you stay awhile you'll be borne along,
Become one with the moods of the bay.

The fishermen sing as they haul in their nets
Sweet winds and bobbing sails beckon me,
and gulls croon to a watery melody
On lovely Chedabucto Bay.

I've felt the power and the fury,
The tides of Tranquillity;
I share a kinship with these waters
And the breakers of the bay.

When of city strife I weary
Sure my hungry heart will stray
towards the sweet winds of Canso
On the shores of Chedabucto Bay.

2

As Laurie was lulled by the pleasant rocking of the train and her aunt Lena read, she thought about how different life had been with her grandmother. At home there were always complaints about her behaviour. Though Jamie, her dad, spoke to her gently enough most of the time, sometimes he yelled, so that Laurie was afraid of him. Her mother, Serafina, made it quite obvious that she didn't like her.

Laurie felt as if she was to blame for everything that went wrong. She was told she was too curious, too fussy, and a host of other faults were attributed to her, the main one being that she was, as Mother said, " born with a silver spoon in your mouth." Laurie knew it had something to do with the fact that she objected vociferously to dirty clothes or anything dirty for that matter. She hated to use a spoon or a cup that someone else had used before it was washed, something that she was often forced to do. She disliked fatty foods, especially her mother's minestrone, because it had greasy rings floating on top. Just the smell made her feel sick.

Laurie was accused of touching things from the china cabinet when she was little and breaking them. Serafina saved all the broken pieces. Sometimes she would open the bottom drawer of the buffet and say, "Look at what you broke, all because you're too darn nosey." Why didn't she lock the cabinet and hide the key, Laurie wondered? It *had* a key. And why did she save the pieces?

Serafina would tell everyone stories about how bad Laurie was when she was three or four years old. According to her, Laurie thought, I was the only one who misbehaved when I was little, but she did say that everyone thought I was cute. Apparently, I lisped, so the policemen taught me to say, "Come up and thee me thum time," just like Mae West.

Laurie also thought about Edna, the maid they once had, who was kind to her. A simple country girl with a pleasant disposition, she sang as she ironed, "She'll be comin' round the mountain when she comes," along with a medley of hillbilly tunes. It seemed to make her work lighter and it entertained them as well. For the few years she was with them the apartment was in order and Laurie always had something clean to wear. She left just when Laurie started school, when she needed her the most.

As Laurie's thoughts dwelled on the past, a strange feeling of apprehension and excitement seeped into her, for though she was eager to see her family, she had reason to be nervous, especially where Serafina was concerned.

It had been four months since Laurie had seen her mother. She loved her and longed to cuddle up to her. Maybe it would happen, she thought. Maybe Mother really missed me because I've been away so very long. She recalled how, once, she was sitting on her lap, encircled in her arms, with her head on her chest. A warmth had flooded through her. She wanted to stay there a while longer to savour the sensation but was pushed away. It was a brief experience but she longed for it to happen again. Sadly, this was not to be.

And she thought about her dad, Jamie. He was an enigma. Soft-spoken and gentle most of the time, especially when anyone was sick, he was rarely verbally abusive, but when angry, he resembled a madman. His children would stay clear lest he box their ears or give them a whack on the head. He didn't like noise or yelling, not even a happy noise, if it got too loud.

He had very definite ideas about what was important. Oranges were very important (in the days of the Depression they were lucky to have them), as well as porridge, brown bread and cream of wheat. Molasses was so important, he said, that it was mentioned in the Bible. Laurie hated molasses!

According to Jamie, life without a dog was not really living, just like life without fishing and hunting was some kind of martyrdom. He always had a cocker spaniel until he discovered Labrador retrievers. He said a Labrador was just about the only dog that could love a man almost like a human.

One day, while looking through the Montreal *Star* ads for a dog, he finally found the one he wanted but couldn't afford the price. "It's a bit beyond my means," he said to the vendor, "can you possibly sell it for less," whereupon the man humiliated him. In a nasty way, he told Jamie that he had better buy a cat. After Jamie hung up, he became enraged.

"How dare he speak to me like that!" he said, "I'll fix him!" He dialled again and in a very pleasant voice asked if there was a dog for sale. When the man replied that yes, he had a real gem of a dog, Jamie said in no uncertain terms, "Well then, shove him up your ass," and slammed down the receiver. Serafina was gesticulating in the background. With a loud whisper, she said, "no Jamie, no!" and covered her mouth, feigning shock. But Laurie noticed that she had a twinkle in her eye.

Laurie laughed out loud at the memory so that some of the passengers looked at her curiously. She pretended to have a coughing fit and looked out of the window.

It was a very long journey from Canso to Montreal, and after crossing Chedabucto Bay to Mulgrave, mostly by train. Laurie had a lot of time for thinking and to prepare the transition from one world into another. She mostly remembered.

St Laurent 1931

The dark enclosed itself upon her, enveloping her in terror. Instinctively, she pulled the blankets over her head. Laurie's eyes peered from under the covers, irresistibly drawn to the closet door, and the long watch began. The horrors she imagined lurking within its depths began as infinitesimal structures, then grew and grew till they knew no bounds and became so grotesque, so horrific that a tightness filled her chest and every breath became a belaboured gasp. She must, she simply must open the door, just a small ray of light, just a trickle of light was all she needed. But first she must put her feet to the floor, while under the bed was the ever present hand ready to clutch at her ankle. She thought she should surely die of fright. After interminable minutes in which she talked herself into courage that came from some deep well within the recesses of her child's mind, she bounded across the room, her heart pounding in her ears. She returned to her bed trembling and gazed with infinite relief upon that sweet ray of light. She dwelt on it lovingly, and wondered if God, too, was afraid when all was darkness. Surely, He must have been, she reasoned, this is why he first created light.

Slowly, she began to relax, hearing distant voices, or perhaps a radio, the ordinary everyday sounds that reassured her and assuaged her fears. But no sooner would her father walk down the hall and see the door ajar, he would close it again, and all her horrors would commence. This would occur once or twice, or a third time, till at last, all her energies consumed in fear, she slept.

So vivid was the memory of such a night that she almost bolted from her seat when Lena tapped her on the shoulder to get her attention. She said it was lunch time and gave Laurie a sandwich. Aunt Lena, engrossed in her novel, read as she ate. As Laurie slowly chewed, her thoughts turned to more pleasant things. She remembered her brother.

Murdo was a year older than Laurie, but it was he she played with more often than her sister Catherine who was a year younger. They would put on skits. He would be L'il Abner and she would be Daisy Mae, and they would create their own comic strips. Murdo had more imagination than Catherine, and as an added attraction he played with boys. They sometimes let Laurie tag along. She had decided that boys were more interesting than girls. They didn't care about what she wore but accepted her as she was. When they played cowboys and Indians, they all agreed that a nurse would come in handy, and when they built their snow forts, they let her put in the finishing touches like tables and shelves, and supply them with plenty of snowball ammunition for their battles.

Once when she was five years old she followed them across Décarie into a wooded area. Some boys asked her to pull down her panties so they could see what a girl looked like. "We don't have sisters," they said, "C'mon, do us a favour, be a good sport."

"I will if you give me your licorice," Laurie replied.

Once she had it safely in her pocket, she quickly pulled her panties down and then up again, so fast that they were unable to get a good look. She then ran for all she was worth, their outraged cries of "no fair, no fair" following her.

To this day licorice holds a special significance for her, albeit a humorous one, a ploy of the devil and the first step on the road to prostitution.

Laurie knew nothing about anatomy or the facts of life. Eventually when she tackled the sixth commandment in grade two, there was mention of impure thoughts and impure touches. Wondering why anyone would want to touch their "privates," as Mother referred to them, she had some vague idea that it had something to do with hygiene. It was many years before she was to solve the mystery of the impure touch. In the meantime she followed the rules that were spelled out in the Catechism.

However, it was not the Catechism with its strict regulations that sparked her spirituality, but her mother, for she read her *Robinson Crusoe* and, of more significance, the first poem she had ever heard, *Trees* by Joyce Kilmer. Trees were plentiful then; you could see them everywhere, tall and shady, old and perfect. She contemplated them, along with the words of the poem, and felt a stirring in her soul. She sensed that not everyone felt this stirring because Murdo and Catherine weren't impressed, nor did they memorize the poem as she did.

Laurie again savoured the fondest memory she had of her mother, that evening long ago when she read the entire story of Robinson Crusoe as she sat at the kitchen table, surrounded by her children. They were eating cooked spaghetti straight from the pot with their fingers, because they would not let her stop reading long enough to heat the sauce. It was a spellbinding, happy evening, and never did spaghetti taste so good.

Although mother read her nursery rhymes and the Sunday comics, she rarely had time for more. But it was enough to create an insatiable desire for books. Laurie was determined to read them all.

She wanted to read now, wondering why nobody had provided her with a book on such a long journey. She leaned her head against the cold pane till she envisioned Serafina's face in the glass against a background of endless trees, beautiful trees that appeared to go on forever, and slipped back into memories of Mother.

Serafina was a tiny fun-loving woman with a good sense of humour. She could look cute in a petite way and sometimes she looked pretty. There was nothing about her that was actually ugly, except for her glasses, which were very thick. Her nose was not a lovely nose but neither was it too big. Her lips were thin, but she had a warm smile. Her best feature was her skin which was perfection and remained comparatively free of wrinkles well into old age. She also remained slim throughout her life.

Serafina watched Laurie as she played alone, talking to her dolls. What was she up to now?—making a hospital, she had said. Last month she had emptied the walk-in closet and built a kitchen in there, and another time it was a beauty parlour. She must admit that the girl did have a knack for making things out of just about anything. The girl had imagination and would spend hours playing alone. Serafina didn't think this normal, and thought her daughter to be in some way antisocial or unlikeable.

Jamie's crazy about her, Serafina thought. It was always Laurie he asked about as soon as he came home from work. He made a fuss over her, especially when she was younger.

Serafina remembered how it was when she and Jamie were first married and even when they were alone with Murdo. When he came home he would sit her on his lap and call her his little Snookie. He brought her flowers and chocolates. She would always have a pretty dress on and cologne. He had eyes only for her. But now she was pregnant again and felt awful. She was sick of wearing wraparounds and her hair had lost its shine. She had tried one of those new permanent waves, which had made her hair even worse, like straw. Seeing her daughter's thick shiny hair, she felt strangely annoyed.

"Laurie, your hair needs doing, c'mere."

"Not now Mommy, please! I combed it myself. I don't like braids."

"Braids are the easiest to care for and they suit you just fine, come here!" Laurie approached reluctantly.

Laurie didn't like it when her mother did her hair because she pulled too hard. She made the braids so tight that they hurt. When she complained and tried to get away, mother got annoyed and yanked her back. She dreaded having her hair washed too, because she had to lean back under the bath taps and the water would pour into her eyes. If the soap got into her eyes, making her yell, Serafina would get angry. It felt as if she would yank her hair out.

Once at a time like this, when she cried, Grandma Dolores came to her rescue. Shouting at Serafina, she shooed her out of the bathroom and proceeded to wash Laurie's hair herself. Laurie, feeling the difference in her gentle touch, relaxed under her soothing ministrations and her loving words. Suddenly, she realized that this was the way it was supposed to be.

Laurie thought her grandma Dolores talked funny because she couldn't pronounce her g's. She would say she would have ekks for breakfast and she called the king the kink. She was Maltese. She would never let Laurie cry, for she knew just what to say to make her smile again. The girl loved her. But her grandmother lived in New York and though she stayed for long visits, she wasn't always there to rescue Laurie.

She told Laurie about Malta, and it sounded like a paradise.

"You can go into de garden and pick fiks [figs] or apricots," she said, and "it iss never too cold like Canada. It iss an island in de sea and der iss blue water everywhere. Alvays der iss a feast day…such fun de feast days, wid dancing in der streets and de firecrockers in de sky."

It was also a sad story, because she told Laurie that her husband Salvatore had died when the children were very young. It was her oldest son who immigrated to the United States, saved his money and sent passage for the whole family, all six of them. She told about Ellis Island and how Serafina almost didn't get through because her eyesight was so poor. What she didn't tell Laurie was that two of her babies had died. Laurie guessed it was too sad for her to talk about. Laurie wanted to go to Malta but Nana said it was too far away.

"When you start school," she said, "ask de teacher to show you where Malta iss on de map. Der will be a large map on de wall."

Nana, her eyes bright with love, looked down at Laurie. She will be a great beauty, Nana thought, …then wishing somehow to protect her, she said: " I hope you know dat iff you look in de mirror for too lonk, you will see de devil."

Laurie believed Nana. Once she thought she spied something from the corner of her eye while posing, and for a time avoided mirrors altogether. Nana didn't realize just how very sensitive Laurie was. She would have been upset had she known that she had caused the girl such fear.

Jamie, Laurie's dad, said that Grandma Dolores was a Saint. Laurie was curious. The saints she saw in holy pictures had sad faces like Basset hounds with eyes rolled up heavenwards and arms stretched out as if to say, "sorry, no more potatoes." They also performed miracles.

"Why is Grandma a Saint, Daddy?"

"Because she gives everything she has and never complains," he said.

Nana Dolores radiated a happiness which was not dependent on circumstances, but rather a special kind of joy that was contagious. Her gentleness, her empathy and understanding, her love and inner joy shone from her eyes. To look into those eyes, and to talk to her, was somehow to be a better person, changed and full of hope. It is as though she had tapped the secret of life. She was ill for years and in pain, but except for the occasional 'ajma' [i-ma], the expression of pain that Laurie heard coming from her bedroom at night, she never complained. She was a happy woman, a truly religious person, who reached out to embrace another's reality as part of a universal Faith. This was Nana Dolores; God smiled his love from her eyes. Memories, memories! ...

Early school days steeped in religion: never ending prayers, trips in groups for confession, the way of the cross, Benediction, and all manner of occasions for going to church, the chief one being High Mass on Sundays.

Laurie sat with the rest of the class and tried not to fidget as the Gregorian chanting went on and on. She became mesmerized and sleepy, only to awaken with a jolt as the priest ranted from the pulpit. It was at these times that she wished she understood French. The pastor was always angry about something. She was curious to know which of the commandments were being broken. Everything seemed to be a sin. You had to be "as perfect as your heavenly Father was perfect," or so Sister said.

On the walls of the school corridors were very large oil paintings of Dante's *Inferno*. They were lurid in detail: naked bodies broiling in flames that somehow just managed to cover their genitals, vicious devils serving platters of snakes, some forcing them down into the throats of the sinners with pitchforks. Laurie wondered how anybody could be so bad as to end up there!

Laurie's father helped her with catechism homework. Being a Baptist, he found it very interesting. She remembered his droning voice as he asked her the questions:

"Who is God?"

"God is the creator of Heaven and of Earth and of all things."

"Who made God?"

"God always was and always will be."

His favourite commandment was "Honour thy father and thy mother." It required instant obedience without question, not only to parents but to teachers and anyone else in authority. He liked *that* and thought the Catholic religion was not doing his children any harm.

Although Laurie was good at Catechism and a good reader, spelling out loud for her father was a lot harder than doing it on paper. When she made the same mistake more than once, he raised his voice and his face looked angry. She could not handle anger, would tense up and misspell a word that she had right moments before. Then he would yell, "The girl's stupid," and vent his frustration. It was at this point that she usually wet her pants.

Once she started school, she soon realized that she did not look the same as other children. Her clothes were too large so that she could grow into them, and not always clean, and her stockings were always falling down. She rarely felt good about her appearance. Remarks such as, "Is that your grandmother's grenfel?" or "You wa-ash your ha-air once a ye-ear" by school-mates in group singalong were a common occurrence. She was always to remember in every detail those unkind jibes that she wished she could forget. Her snow jacket, though new, was several sizes too big. As for her hair, it was usually dirty since the maid Edna had left. She started to wash her own hair when she became infested with lice. After complaining about the itch to her mother every night for many weeks, it was her dad who finally investigated and proclaimed, "the girl's lousy." He was the one who phoned the doctor and gave her treatments. He would also sit for many an hour nit-picking. Throughout the whole business, Serafina refused to go near her.

Since the girls she tried to be friendly with wouldn't have her, Laurie turned to those less popular and less fortunate than her. In those days of the depression some were extremely poor. Jane Mullen had a father who sat on a wooden box in the back yard, weaving back and forth and slurring his threats as he beat a whip on the dusty ground. His children would laugh and yelp and run for cover. Laurie went there only once and was afraid to go again.

She then went to the store with a friendly Polish girl, Sophie, who had beautiful pale blond hair. Since she bought chicken feed, Laurie was hoping to see baby chicks. When she went to her home, however, it was far out of town to a run-down farm. Her parents avoided coming out to meet Laurie, nor did they invite her in, but scolded through the screen door in Polish. It was apparent that the girl had done the wrong thing in bringing someone home, and although Laurie had made the long trip only to be made unwelcome, it was Sophie she felt sorry for.

Laurie learned something from these associations, namely that poverty is a relative thing. She also gave up seeking friendships, and reverted once more to playing alone. Since there wasn't much about school to be happy about, she looked forward to Fridays.

It was on Friday evenings, after supper, that she went with her brother Murdo to the basement of the Protestant school. There, for five cents, they watched a serial movie, *Tarzan of the Apes*. He was the idol of her life, and when Jane came on the scene, Laurie of course fantasized about being in her place. She lived for Friday nights.

The radio was also a source of pleasure. They would sit quietly, she and Murdo, with their ears glued to it. If she was lucky enough to be unobserved, once in a while, she stayed up later to be scared out of her wits by the "Inner Sanctum," a horror story that left a lot to her imagination, which, even then, was all too well developed.

One day Laurie came home to find a titanic woman in the kitchen. She was the new maid, Bernie. She spoke only a few words of English, being part French and part North American Indian. She had a swarthy complexion and a smile for everyone. When her brother Jimmy, who was still young enough to be very outspoken, came home, he managed not to make any remarks about her girth—that is, until he couldn't get past her in the hall, whereupon he said, "You're so fat you block the hall." Furious, she made it quite plain that she would not tolerate any remarks about her weight.

Once Bernie was late coming home from Mass. Serafina sent Jimmy to fetch her at the soda bar, where she hung out with the local "yokels." At first he couldn't see her, so he went up to the counter and asked the proprietor in a loud voice, loud enough for everyone to hear, "Where's big apples?"

She came home chasing Jimmy, if you can call it chasing. Rather she waddled as fast as she could, her voluminous breasts bouncing up and down, her face an angry red, perspiring profusely, and muttering every possible profanity. Though Jimmy was chastised, he was more entertained than punished because he could see everyone was trying not to laugh. Bernie was with the Moffatts for only a few months. She was a cheerful sort but often more of a hindrance than a help.

As it turned out, it was Laurie's teacher, Sister Gonzaga, who helped her. She was a tiny little nun, with the face of an angel, and the ugliest name Laurie had ever heard. There was a time when the girl was afraid of her.

One day Laurie looked up from her desk and noticed to her acute embarrassment that the class was all stationed at the blackboard. Sister was waiting with folded arms, her lips pressed into an angry thin line. The poor girl sauntered up slowly to save face, and this angered the nun. After school she took her into the cloakroom, pulled down her pants and spanked her. It didn't hurt much but the humiliation of having her see Laurie's bare bottom was punishment enough.

It was after the long illness of scarlet fever that Laurie arrived at school, late as usual. She stood at the classroom door dressed in winter clothing, enveloped in a scarf with only a small portion of her face visible, in a state of complete bewilderment. There had been a room change in her absence and she was wondering if she was in the right place.

Sister came running toward her, arms outstretched, laughing with delight. She lifted Laurie onto her lap and kissed her repeatedly as she removed her outer clothing. Laurie's fear of her vanished. She knew that Sister really loved her for she actually had tears in her eyes. Sister Gonzaga was the essence of charity and cared for her pupils as she would have had they been her own children.

Laurie was often involved in some sort of difficulty from which Sister would rescue her. Since Serafina was not the most efficient of homemakers, her two daughters were nearly always late for school in the morning.

"Hurry Catherine, we'll be late again." said Laurie.

"I can't run any faster, I have a pain in my side."

"So have I, but we can't stop now."

They arrived panting to find the doors locked. " We're too late, now we'll get it!" Laurie said. She rang the bell and awaited the principal, a nun of imposing stature and very strict countenance. When she appeared, her face a mask of anger, to heap recriminations upon them, Laurie understood not a word, as the tirade was in French. And yet, quaking inside, she could feel the urine run down her legs as she wet her pants with fright. She was held responsible for their insistent tardiness as her sister Catherine was younger. Laurie, being much taller as well, bore the brunt of her anger.

The next time Laurie found herself in the same situation she conceived of a daring plan. "C'mon Cath," she said, and ran to the back of the building under her classroom window.

"Sister, Sister," she called in an anguished semi-whisper. When this didn't achieve the desired effect, she threw a few small pebbles at her window. Sister Gonzaga finally came into view, assessed the situation, unbarred the door and sneaked them, tip-toeing, into the classroom unobserved.

Then there was the time she dressed Jane Mullen. Jane hadn't been to school for over a week. Sister asked if anyone knew if she was ill. "Jane can't come to school because she has nothing to wear but her bathing suit," Laurie said. "That's what she told me when I saw her riding down the street on a bicycle yesterday."

From that day onwards, Sister dressed Jane Mullen when she came to school and removed her clothes before she left. They were always washed and ironed, ready and waiting for her. Laurie wondered why she couldn't wear them home and supposed it was because they might be given to someone else in the family.

Sister Gonzaga's pockets fascinated Laurie. She just never knew what was in those roomy pockets that reached way down to her little feet. One day it was a cookie or a candy and another day a ribbon for someone's hair, a ball or a skipping rope. Once she produced a dry change of underwear for Laurie.

And so, Laurie's early school days consisted mainly of trying to get there on time, fear of rejection, worry about Math, worry that her stockings would finally fall to her ankles as she walked, trying not to wet her pants before getting home, but failing miserably.

These were the reveries of a nine-year-old girl with large, expressive, and sometimes sad-looking eyes, till the train pulled into Windsor Station in Montreal.

When Laurie arrived home and told everyone about her stay in Canso with such obvious delight, her dad was the one who listened hungrily. He had missed the girl and felt extremely pleased to discover that she shared his love for his home town.

He loved Canso, but there was no work there since the depression. He had a good job with Bell when most people were out of work. First the single men were laid off, then the men with one or two children. Soon men with three or even four children were being laid off. Since Serafina was expecting her fifth, they were saved. Her being a Catholic had in a way saved him his job, he thought wryly. Since he had a wife and four children, soon to be five, dependent on him, the best he could do when he hankered for the wild was to go on an occasional hunting or fishing trip. But this no longer satisfied him, so he had taken steps to move his family to a place where he knew he could be happy.

3

St Lambert, 1936

When they moved to St Lambert in the Spring, there before Laurie was the St Lawrence River in all its pristine beauty. It was as if God knew where she wanted to be. In the background was St Helen's Island, a picture of romance with its tower high above the trees. But it was the smaller Moffatt's Island which held a special fascination for her. She had wished for an island just last summer when out on the bay with Captain Simms, knowing of course it was just a wish, and one did not expect a wish like that to come true. Yet here was an island that bore her name. She had no doubt whatever that God had something to do with it, because it seemed like a miracle.

Treeless, it clung tenaciously to the river just above the roaring rapids, a sanctuary for a variety of birds that decked the skies, and then boisterously proclaimed their territorial imperative from its rocky shores. Often when she watched the sun scatter flame upon the evening water and slowly sink behind the purple tops of Mt Royal, she would ponder the mystery of the island that bore her name. To some day brave the strong current above the rapids and go there, she knew somehow, was to fulfil her destiny.

In the meanwhile, St Lambert was country living at its best. Here, as in Canso, nature revealed her secrets to Laurie. It was a place to reap happy childhood memories, memories she was to hold close in her heart. There were any number of exciting events that summer, but of more significance was the boy next door, David Walker. So full of animation and zest for life was he, there weren't enough hours in a day, and he made no secret of the fact that he was crazy about Laurie. He would come to the kitchen window and signal her to come outside. She would pretend to have finished her homework and fly to his side. It was hard to resist his snapping black eyes, as he was a handsome boy and extremely good-natured.

Then he would very masterfully lead her to the swing, stand in front of her holding on to the ropes, and looking down at her, sing love songs, mostly about her eyes. He actually made them up as he went along and she felt dizzy with his unabashed adoration.

This was pretty potent stuff for someone of such a tender age and hard to handle. Since David might see her at any time, keeping herself spotless and washing her long hair, which she now wore loose, was time-consuming but necessary. Someone gave Serafina a box of second-hand clothing and in it Laurie found a white cotton skirt. It fit her perfectly and she would wash and iron it by hand nearly every day.

That summer was a happy one for Laurie, but in September David said, "Let's show how much we love each other by the number of petals left on a daisy." Removing all the petals from his, he handed her a yellow centre on a stem. She handed him her daisy intact, which made him uncomfortable, and then he said sheepishly, "We can't get married anyway, because you're a Catholic."

As she lay on her bed that night, Laurie thought about what he had said. It was all very well to learn Catechism but this was real life! It was the first time she was sorry that she was a Catholic and she felt guilty about her feelings. Did boys lie about how they felt? She had no answers to any of her questions. When she queried her mom and dad, they laughed and called it "puppy love." She couldn't understand how they could laugh when she felt so bad.

Weeping, she got up and took a little tin of treasures from the closet shelf. In it were some very beautiful Christmas cards, a snow white rabbit's tail, some marbles so pretty that she couldn't bear to use them, and the seashell that Tom had given her in Canso. She clutched the little shell and wished she was there again on the cliffs with Tom. He hadn't said he loved her, like David had many times, but he never made her feel unhappy.

"Some day when I'm older, I'll go back and see you again, Tommy," she said aloud, "and I'll keep your shell forever." This was when Laurie decided to write to him, wondering why she had not thought of it before. Taking a page from her notebook, she began.

Dear Tommy,

I guess you will be surprised to get this letter. Next month, I will be ten.

We moved to St Lambert in May. It is on the shore of the St Lawrence River. Guess what? There is an Island named Moffatt's Island and a beach where I can have swimming lessons.

Last week Murdo and I found tadpoles in a pond. They are in a jar in the back porch. Dad said they are baby frogs and will grow legs.

Sometimes there is a band concert in Gordon Park, and after it is over they show cartoon movies. In the winter there will be sleigh rides.

I like it much better here than in St Laurent

because it is more like being in the country. We picked a big bowl of wild strawberries. There are lots of chokecherry bushes. I ate too many and got the hives. I nearly itched to death but they are gone now.

I guess your shell collection is much larger now. I still have the one you gave me. I miss you and I would be very pleased if you would write me a letter.

Goodbye for now,
your friend, Laurie

P.S. I hope you are not sad any more.

Writing the letter made her feel better somehow. She did not feel confident enough to expect an answer, having learned that feelings changed. Perhaps, she thought, Tom had forgotten about her. After all, he was now thirteen and starting high school...and there was the girl with the nice soft voice...

Luckily, she and David remained friends throughout her stay on Notre Dame Street. He allowed her in his gang as the much-needed nurse for their battles, or as an admiring observer as he played with his soldiers. They would chat as he set up barricades made with old dried tea sacs, which resembled sandbags. She loved to listen to his sound effects: pow! Rat-tat-tat! neowh! chew! pfoo!

Often he would sit on the curb, surrounded by several of the neighbourhood children, Laurie included, creating a tale of mystery and intrigue. They were spellbound as he took them through caves and secret corridors, trap doors and escape routes. He was a master storyteller.

And so Laurie learned a very important fact of life, namely, that someone could like you a lot, even after they stopped loving you.

It was at this time that another maid, Rita, came into the picture very briefly. Serafina gave her permission to go for a swim and she was to take Laurie with her. The girl was delighted to discover the beach, with its well-defined boundaries, one for girls and the other for boys. She liked to watch the older experienced swimmers springing from the board in graceful dives, or belly flopping for the fun of it. The rocky shores of Lake Megantic had hurt her feet and the water was too deep, but this was different. The bottom was sandy and the water was just up to her waist at one point. Laurie soon learned how to swim.

All went well that day until they were walking home. Two boys on bicycles followed them and struck up a conversation with the maid. One of them was really good-looking. Laurie couldn't understand what they saw in Rita, as she looked rather a slattern with her stringy, greasy-looking hair.

"Why are they following us?" she asked."

"Because I put a note in their towel."

"What did the note say?"

"Would you like to fuck?"

Laurie didn't know exactly what the word meant. She was told once that it meant what dogs did. She saw them jumping up on top of each other but when she tried to get closer to investigate they always ran off. It had looked like some kind of rubbing. She was shocked because everyone knew it was a dirty word. Once her dad had washed out Jimmy's mouth with soap for saying it. Now Rita had said it right out loud without any embarrassment whatsoever.

Before Laurie could say more, the cute boy approached her, and asked if she was a Catholic. She said "No," because she was afraid he would think Catholic girls were bad, whereupon the maid was horrified.

When they got home, she turned on Laurie. "You denied your faith," she said, "so you committed a terrible sin! How could you do such a thing?"

"Because I was ashamed of what you did," Laurie replied, in a state of complete bewilderment. She wondered if indeed she had done something terrible and wondered why Rita was not worried about her own sin... or was it a sin?

Another day Rita told Murdo, who was now ten, and Laurie that her boyfriend had a big dick, and proceeded to show them just how large with her hands. Laurie asked her what a dick was, and she pointed between Murdo's legs. "You mean a diddely dander," the girl said, "but you're just fooling us because diddely danders are little things. Anyway, if your boyfriend let you see his, then he's a pig, and you both should go to confession."

Luckily for them, the maid was lazy, and had to go before the month was up. If she had not, there was no telling what sort of an education she would have given them.

That winter Serafina decided that Laurie and her sister Catherine were to be boarders in the Convent of the Holy Names down the street. This was the most miserable experience of Laurie's childhood. Except for her classroom teacher, the nuns spoke very little English, and to make matters worse, Laurie feared them.

The convent itself was a pleasure to see with its waxed and polished hardwood floors. Delicate ferns on wooden pedestals graced every window and the nuns made sure that none of the pupils ever touched them. Most rooms were large and all of them spotlessly clean.

The uniforms the girls wore were black wool serge with tiny pleats down the front to the waist. Every week they had to remove a thin, lace-bordered cotton collar by picking out the stitches; they then washed it and sewed it back on. Thick black stockings and black shoes completed the outfit. For special occasions they wore a replica in white with a large sash tied in a bow at the back and white stockings.

Laurie liked the gym uniform she wore once a week. It was a white and navy middy blouse, the same kind that sailors wore, and a navy pleated skirt. It suited her and disguised her bony frame.

Life here revolved around bells, gongs and clackers. The clackers looked like square castanets. They were held in one hand and when a nun clacked, it was a signal to rise and line up, or to sit down. Another clack and the line proceeded single file and in complete silence to their destination. The bells were either large ones that the sisters swung back and forth vigorously so they could be heard at a considerable distance, or small ones that tinkled when used solely for one large room.

In the morning the girls awakened with a bell. They poured water from a pitcher into a basin, washed their faces and hands, and brushed their teeth. This done, they proceeded to the washroom to empty and clean their basin. Soon another bell signalled that it was time to remove their arms from the sleeves of their long flannelette nightgowns. With their arms inside as in a tent, they put on their underwear. With the next bell they were expected to be fully clothed in uniform. The older girls in secondary school had curtains around their cubicles. They were at the other end of the dormitory and the bells signalled the opening and the closing of their curtains.

Laurie's cubicle consisted of a narrow iron bed, a washstand and a chair. She combed her hair, tidied up and made her bed before the next bell. Nobody dared not be ready and they stood waiting like soldiers when the clack signalled them to proceed in single file to the chapel, leaving the dormitory in perfect order with rows of spotless white bedspreads.

All this was done without a word or a whisper, for to talk in the dorm was more serious and open to suspicion than to talk anywhere else. The sleeping areas and the bathrooms were considered haunts of the devil where the girls might be subjected to all sorts of temptations. What they thought they could have done in such a strict environment was beyond Laurie's comprehension. They were watched like hawks, a nun guarding the interior of every washroom with folded arms and stern face, as if to challenge even a whisper.

Saturday night was bath night. The tub areas were enclosed, and how Laurie loved to see and feel the walls around her. This was the only privacy made possible. She lingered for as long as possible.

A few of the girls discussed in whispers once, outside in the playground, about how funny it would be, if they could see one of the nuns in a bath. One girl said she had been sent to a different section once because the cubicles were all full. "I peeked over the top of her booth. The nun was sitting in the tub with her underwear on. Her head was all shaved."

"Maybe the nun was cold," Laurie said, for she couldn't imagine a situation where someone would consider their body evil or dirty, something to be hidden from even her own eyes.

Every morning after mass, which thankfully was not a long one, they were clicked and clacked to the refectory for a breakfast of dry cereal, a bun with peanut butter and a glass of milk. Then the bell sounded and they were clacked to their course. The course was the leisure or play area reserved for grades one to six. The proper word was really cours, a French word, but course was in general use by the English. The older girls had a separate course divided from theirs by massive folding walls, the same as those used in hotels.

There were only a handful of English who were boarders, the rest being day pupils. Laurie was the only one in her grade level, her sister and one other being in a level below hers and three others in grades one and two. The rest, about forty in all, were French and couldn't speak any English. The course nun, or Supervisor, knew a few words, but it seemed only enough to scold or deride. She certainly was no mother substitute, which the girls needed desperately.

Laurie had her own small cupboard with a colouring book and crayons, paper dolls and whatever they had brought from home for playtime activities. She loved paper dolls and enjoyed them until the nun made her throw them away. "They have no clothes," she said.

"But," Laurie argued, "they have to be wearing only their underwear so they can be dressed." She proceeded to demonstrate, but the nun was adamant.

Laurie rarely played with her sister Catherine, as she was much younger in her ways. Catherine took to playing with a girl named Beverly who was younger still. The French girls stuck together. They had no interest in playing with "les tannantes Anglaises," as they were referred to. The literal translation meant "the sickening or maddening English," but they were told that it meant "English pests." Laurie spent long hours with her colouring book. By the end of the school year she was probably a master at the art of colour selection.

She also had a reading hour when she sat in a hard chair with a small desk in front of her, in complete silence. This was her favourite time, because when she read she could be somewhere else for just a little while in her imagination and life did not seem so bad.

The meals were adequate but there was no fruit on the table. Parents were to bring the fruit on visiting days, but since Laurie never saw hers, she could only watch the others eat.

Weekends at the convent, which should have been a time for relaxation, Laurie would anticipate with her heart in her mouth. She longed to see her parents, but especially her mother. Visiting hours were Saturday and Sunday afternoon from two till four. Home being just down the street, Laurie would lean out of the window waiting for a glimpse of Mother.

There were some girls whose parents were impossibly far away, who couldn't get there, but many visited from Montreal and outlying areas. Laurie's lived a block away and never came to see her.

She tried to play but couldn't. Even when it became apparent that no one was coming, she kept her vigil at the window, "just in case," and cried her heart out. She could not phone home nor did she receive any calls. The nun in charge usually mocked her when she cried. She called her "Mater Dolorosa," which meant "Mother of Sorrows."

Laurie looked at her and she knew then that a nun was not always good nor holy. Sister could have comforted her to a certain degree. She could have shared her heartache and thereby scored points with her Jesus, but instead she put a fine edge to the girl's pain.

But there was a sister who had a sunny disposition. In the Spring, she would let Laurie have a stalk of rhubarb from her wheelbarrow. The girl would peek in the basement scullery and see the plump, rosy-cheeked little nun peeling vegetables. She thought that she would hate working all day in that damp and cheerless place, and yet this sister always had a smile and a twinkle in her eye.

Laurie thought that had she been dressed in red and white instead of black she would have made a perfect wife for Santa Claus. She was a true Religious, a saintly person.

It seemed strange to Laurie that Catherine didn't care when nobody came to visit her, nor was she adversely affected by her convent stay. She would simply revert to thumb-sucking with a glazed expression on her face. Of course Catherine did care, but she had no expectations as Laurie had, nor was she mature enough to consider the implications of the situation.

They went home for Christmas, but by the time summer arrived, Laurie was a changed person. She had felt abandoned and unloved. Her nature was such that normally she bounced back easily, but this time she did not. Gone was the carefree child and in her place was a serious and introspective young adult.

There were boys in the convent but in only the lower grades, and they lived in another part of the building. Their dining area was separated by a folding wall.

Once Laurie had the audacity to make a face at her food and was seen by the nun who sat at the head of her table. As her punishment, she was made to sit and eat this food in the presence of all the boys, who stared at her throughout the meal. She wasn't upset about this – rather, she was glad to see boys again as she was beginning to forget what they looked like.

Laurie was by now a devout Catholic because in her mind God was the only one who loved her. Because nobody hugged her, she turned to the spirit in sublimation. She would talk to Jesus and Mary often, that is, until St Joseph entered her life.

Her teacher said that he wasn't really the father of Jesus and yet he took care of Him. Nobody made a fuss over St Joseph. This lowly carpenter seemed neglected. Everyone prayed to the other saints and to Mary. She suddenly felt an affinity for him. They were both alone.

The one thing Laurie wanted desperately from her course supervisor was an honour ribbon. Any girl who got over ninety percent in conduct at the end of a month could wear a red taffeta moire ribbon draped across her chest and back, and folded at the side. She had an occasional classroom medal pinned to her uniform for the highest monthly mark in classroom conduct, English, Composition or History, and nearly always for Religion. But the year was nearly over and she had never had an honour ribbon. She was now determined to get one.

Some of the French girls were very chatty with the nun and well liked. They had no trouble getting a ribbon, but for Laurie to get one she knew she had to be much better in ways that would be noticeable. Her conduct was above reproach by even the best of standards, but this was not enough. She knew what to do and St Joseph would help her. She began to pray to him and continued to pray for his help regularly during the day.

When she walked in single file with the rest of the girls, she did so with her hands straight at her sides. Not even once would she so much as whisper a word to anyone after a bell or a clack. She looked straight ahead so that it might not even appear that she might have, not from point A to point B, or from B to C. And never would she be caught crying under any circumstances.

When she sat in a chair to listen to prayers or lectures, she would look straight ahead with her hands folded in her lap. She would look more fervent in demeanour, even look as if she understood French.

When she saw nuns coming up the stairs as she was going down and vice-versa, she would shrink to the rail immobile till they had passed, even more in advance than was required.

The day came at the end of the month when the honour roll was called out. All the girls sat in their appointed chair in the order of their mark for the previous month, the girl with the highest mark in the first chair and the one with the lowest at the end. When Laurie's name was called, a soft echo of a surprised "oh" went down the line as she moved up to the top ten. She had made it! St Joseph had answered her prayers.

When all was said and done, however, what good was the honour if she didn't have the ribbon, nor a cent with which to buy one? But St Joseph came through once again. A girl from a higher course, one who spoke English, took pity on her when she saw her crying in the school yard. She had an extra ribbon which was a bit faded and she gave it to her.

How Laurie loved that girl! She was never to forget her kind face. She fortified Laurie's belief, not only in the goodness of people, but in God who would always love her.

The two girls who always sat in the first chairs of the honour role were sisters and always in animated conversation with the course supervisor during leisure time. They laughed a lot. They were the only girls that were never seen in the dorm. The rumour was that they had a room of their own, because their father was very important, however this was doubtful. That they came from a very well-to-do family was very obvious. They always wore a uniform that looked as if it was being worn for the first time and they wore those classy Red River Coats with red trim, red wool toque, belt and leggings. The French called them Rafers. They also had anything they wanted.

And what about the girls who were always at the end of the honour roll? They obviously could not care less. Laurie cared too much, and played the foolish game against such odds.

The corridor facing Laurie's classroom overlooked the river and Moffatt's Island. She stopped and looked out at every opportunity, and if the window was open, she could hear the gulls and the sound of the rapids until the freeze set in.

She thought about Canso and of how just a year ago she was as free as those birds. Now she felt like a prisoner.

She daydreamed about being with Tommy on Moffatt's Island.

When she went home for Christmas, a card from Tom with a short note awaited her. She must have read it a dozen times. It felt like Manna from Heaven because she thought he was the only person in the world who bothered to think about her. He said that the wind was so cold already that nobody could stay out for very long. He hung around with a gang of school friends. They played hockey on Saturdays and sometimes they went to a dance at Failen Hall. It was the bit about dancing that made Laurie realize how different their lives were. Would she ever go to a dance? They had street dances in the village in summer but she couldn't stay up that late. She knew how to skate though, and took every opportunity to use the small rink in the convent yard.

During the holiday break, she went to a rink near the church with Murdo, and saw a boy and a girl holding hands and skating. They looked so romantic gliding to the music, that is, until the priest came along and made the couple hold opposite ends of hockey stick between them. As soon as the priest left, of course, they were back holding hands and laughing.

Laurie imagined skating with Tom, holding hands that way. She could see his head thrown back in laughter, as she looked up at him, and she felt an agitation within her. It became her favourite fantasy.

She also kept his card hidden from the nuns lest they take it away. Sometimes, in secret, she would kiss it. Her daydreaming helped to make life bearable until the Spring thaw.

Spring, when the ice broke with a roar! The river groaned and snapped like an awakening giant, impatiently throwing off its blanket of ice. Titanic blue translucent floes sailed past the window and crashed one upon the other. The floes were forced towards shore and covered Riverside Drive. More followed, till the street overflowed and they inched precariously near the houses themselves. So awe-inspiring was it to watch that people showed up from all points to witness the spectacle.

Laurie was shaken to her very core! "For yours is the power and the glory," she prayed. This is what it must mean. She took heart, for soon it would be summer again and she could run into the sunshine, see, feel and hear again.

But she must wait awhile yet, if only to dream.

4

Moffatt's Island, 1940

She is on the island not to be alone, but because she is alone. The birds have accepted her. They croon and dive with abandon or observe her quietly as if contemplating the human mystery. There is no noise, only sound. The rapids break in the rocky crevices, gurgle and spume, then rush on like a thunderous ovation to fade in the distance. The sounds comfort her. Nor is it grey or dreary here, even though the island is mainly rock, for there are wild flowers growing among the grasses and some from crevices in the rocks themselves. There is a subtle blending of colour that is slowly perceived, when she half closes her eyes against the sun, as an artist would before dipping a brush, to observe the hidden colour that is there for all to see, if they truly wanted to see it. The pastels become visibly brighter just before sunset, like shy girls becoming bolder with their last chance at radiance.

Sometimes she comes to weep, sometimes to pour her prayer into space. When she leaves she is whole again and filled with peace.

She talks here on the island, sometimes to herself, but mostly to the gull whom she has named Janus for the two-faced Roman God. Aloof, he prefers to perch on his favourite rock and let the breeze run through his feathers. He is young and yet his gull face has a faraway wistful look, a look of longing, as if he were remembering another time. His human side revealed itself to her after she had been talking to him for a long time, at first from a distance. Gradually, he flew in closer to her as she became familiar.

One day when she talked to him as she would a friend, she said, "Janus, I have no breasts. I'm fourteen and there isn't even a hint of them. I read a passage from Daddy's Bible. It says, 'We have a little sister and she hath no breasts; what shall we do for our sister in the day when she shall be spoken for?' I wonder what they did say, Janus. What do you think they said to him? It goes on to say something I just don't understand. 'If she be a wall, we will build upon her a palace of silver; and if she be a door we will enclose her with boards of cedar.' Does it mean that if she stays as flat as a wall or a door they will offer a man money if he will marry her? Suppose I never get breasts. Will it mean that no man will want to marry me? I have never seen anyone my age without them. Why me?"

He turned his head and gave her such a profound and penetrating look as if to say, "why not?" It was his human face, and he looked so funny and so wise that she was taken aback. Till then she used him as she would a sounding board, but now she watched for a response. She felt that he was really listening in some strange way. When he would quickly turn his head and look at her, it always happened to be at a crucial point in her monologue as if to say, "Well then, do it!" or "You said it!" His looks were neither sad nor slow but always an exclamation point. She realized that if she talked enough, she would always answer her own questions, with his prompting; of course. He became her wise counsellor.

To come here for the first time was an act of bravery: she wasn't sure she had the strength to master the current and she was afraid. It happened at a point in her fourteenth year when she sat on the shore and thought about the island's history. It was once called "Isle a la Pierre" or Stone Island. Not only a bird sanctuary, it was a quarry. In 1661, a Father Vignal and thirty-one men, some of them soldiers, had come here to gather stone with which to build a house for the Sisters of Mercy in Ville Marie. Attacked by thirty-five Mohawk and Oneida, hiding in the brush, they all perished.

Nearly two centuries later, George Moffatt bought the island. He had the largest export-import business in Canada, handling a cargo of as many as fifteen foreign ships. How beautiful they must have looked coming down the river, sails billowing in the wind! There remained many unanswered questions, however, and she wondered if the island held some answers.

Suddenly, she knew the time had come. Before she could change her mind, she leaped into her father's boat and cast off. She felt a panic in mid-river when the pull of the current made it harder to row and when the sound of the rapids became a roar in her ears. But once she reached shore, she felt elated and her confidence increased. Now, she was to make frequent trips to what she referred to as "my island." It became not only her second home, but a refuge.

Having reached her maximum height of five feet seven inches too fast, Laurie was noticeably underweight, so that most people remarked on it. She loved clothes, but since they were beyond her reach, she would daydream about them. She knew what type of clothing would help disguise her bony look because she saw the teen magazines, but she wore second-hand clothing most of the time which didn't fit, or accentuated her problem.

One day at the beach a boy pointed to her and said, "look at that freak." Refusing to wear a swimsuit for the rest of the summer, she sat looking over the stone wall above the beach watching what she considered all the *normal* people enjoy the water. She listened to their happy screams and splashes and watched the water stream from their cooled bodies when they climbed onto the dock.

Her sister Catherine was trying to teach Naomi, the youngest, how to swim. They were laughing. Laurie thought Catherine looked about average in a bathing suit. She would have settled for average any time.

There were many girls that she knew, some with mediocre figures and a few with superb figures. The boys vied for their attention. Laurie searched among the bathers. She told herself that if she could find at least two girls as thin as she was, she would put on her bathing suit, but she couldn't find even one. If she could have foreseen that those who looked best would in later years be very overweight, whereas she would look just right, she would have taken heart.

When she went to Saturday night dances at the Protestant school with her two friends Barbara and Dorothy, she mostly held up the wall; some nights she didn't dance even once.

It was at one of these dances that she overheard a few boys talking. "Did you see those big beautiful eyes? Yeah! Wow!" They were laughing. Laurie watched to see who they were talking about. One by one the boys were asking this girl to dance. She wasn't really attractive, being rather obese, nor was she dressed up.

When Laurie mentioned to Dorothy that the boys were talking about the girl's big eyes, she said, "Laurie, you dummy! They aren't talking about her *eyes*. They mean those twenty-inch tits jutting out in front of her." Laurie wondered if the girl knew why she was so popular and felt uncomfortable in the face of what she considered to be a lot of sinning.

And yet, when Murdo told Laurie that she had a figure like two aspirins on an ironing board, she decided to take the necessary drastic measures, and slipped two falsies into her bras, which, as it was, served no purpose except perhaps as a receptacle of hope.

At the next dance, she looked down and to her horror one of them had slipped to her waist. She quickly fled, hopefully before anyone noticed. But she was soon to discover that these tiny parts of her equipment were a source of intense pleasure. At the same time she thought that she had finally discovered the meaning of the impure touch that was mentioned in the Catechism, and which until then had mystified her.

Laurie, having been chastised and sent to her room, took a kitten with her for consolation. Somehow holding and stroking the cat comforted her. She soon dozed with little kitty asleep across her chest. She awoke with the most exquisite pleasure she had ever experienced. The kitten had found her tiny nipple and was sucking like mad. At first she was shocked and removed her, thinking that if she left her she would be guilty of a mortal sin. But she put her back to see if it would happen again. As wave after wave of pleasure engulfed her, she felt that she had discovered what breaking the sixth commandment was all about. This had to be a sin because it felt so-o-o-o goo-ood!

Now she understood why mummy cat looked so happy when her kittens were feeding. She would half close her eyes, purring and languorously stretching, the picture of contentment. She must feel the same as I do six times over!, Laurie thought. "Oh God, she prayed, "let me have breasts, so that some day I will have a baby. Let it suck day and night without my committing a sin."

She let the kitten suck briefly three times, but torn with guilt, she stopped. The guilt was as intense as the pleasure and fraught with complications, because how could she tell a priest about it when she went to confession? It was impossible! The best she could do was to confess to an impure touch and hope he asked her no questions.

And God did spare her, for when she next went to confession, the priest could barely understand English. She mumbled under her breath and he sent her on her way, in a hurry to get back to his reading. She came out of the confessional bathed in sweat; so great was the relief that it felt as if she were walking on air. Ah, what a wonderful catharsis was confession! But she wished for someone to confide in. She wanted to know if she had committed a mortal sin, but just couldn't imagine telling anyone she knew.

Barbara had a scrapbook filled with pictures of hockey stars and listened to all the games on the radio. Dorothy had the walls of her room covered with signed photographs of the movie stars. Both of them went bananas over crooners, but Laurie was not interested in these things.

The best fun she had that summer was raiding apple trees with her brother's friends after dark. Sneaking into a back yard, picking a few apples before the lights went on in the house and a door opened, running for all she was worth and escaping just in time. Eating a few small green sour apples with her fellow pirates and listening to the excited banter. Now that was exhilarating! There were four apple trees in her own back yard, well tended and delicious. But they never tasted as good as the few she swiped on an apple raid.

And she also had a passion for the movies. Whenever she could beg a quarter, she would go and often alone. She didn't need company, being so engrossed as to be a part of the story. She experienced all of the agony while shedding copious tears, and all the ecstasy as the hero wooed her with eyes that would steal her very soul. It was Charlie Chaplin who made her laugh so hard that she would have to go to the ladies' room at intermission, to reinforce her not-so-dry panties with paper towels.

However, it was not easy to get a quarter, so when all was said and done, reading continued to be her favourite pastime. If someone would call her when engrossed in a book, she would not hear. The only way to get her attention was to cover the page and then she would look up with a dazed expression, as if trying to bring herself over the threshold from one world into another.

In the books she fled from reality because the reality was too much to bear. Her home life was so miserable that if she had had some place to escape to, she would have gone without hesitation. Jamie had beaten her many times with a leather belt or a tree switch. This was done at Serafina's insistence. She would give him no peace till she heard Laurie's screams coming from the basement. She and Serafina would have arguments and she was accused of being saucy, which meant she answered back.

On the other hand, her days consisted mostly in seeing to it that her baby sister Lana was not overly neglected and that the house clutter did not reach the point of no return.

Lana was born into what could be called today, a nonfunctional family. Financial resources were stretched to the limit so there never was enough to go around. Laurie often went to bed hungry, not because there was no food in the house, but because she just couldn't stomach what was there.

Catherine filled up on bread slathered with mayonnaise when she came home from school hungry. Just watching her eat it was enough to make Laurie feel sick. She believed it was the source of the many pimples that covered her sister's face. Laurie craved meat and fruit but besides the wild duck that Jamie shot, which she loved with a passion, and apples in the fall, there was very little.

She could never bring herself to complain for it would only accentuate a problem for which there didn't appear to be any solution. She sought rather to make peace at whatever cost.

Nevertheless, she was old enough to consider Serafina's pregnancy with alarm and worried about the outcome. Feeling deeply sorry for that tiny innocent, born into hardship and discord, she felt bound to love and protect her.

Oddly enough, Laurie was the only person in a family of eight who was consistently clean and tidy. This was the most frustrating part of living at home. The adage "a place for everything and everything in its place" was anathema to her family. Coats, hats and mittens were put down anywhere, overshoes scattered near all exits, papers, books and other household paraphernalia were piled on tables and chairs, and as for the kitchen, suffice it to say it disgusted her.

All her efforts at organization and cleanliness were thwarted. Everyone was quite happy to live in squalor, and within a few hours her work was completely undone. She would retire to her corner of the world, half of a bedroom that she shared with Catherine, the tidy half, and face away from the mess. She felt not alone, but lonely.

Often she would leave the house and walk towards the river as if drawn to a magnet. Starved for affection, she longed for a boyfriend. She would see couples on the benches in Gordon Park cuddling and necking, sometimes even in the rain under an umbrella. She wanted a boy to neck the hell out of her, wanted it so badly that she could feel it in her gut.

Though she had not forgotten Tom, she had stopped writing to him over a year ago. Since he had not responded to her letters, she assumed they no longer were of any significance to him. The last time she had heard from him was two years ago at Christmas. His memory was like a piece of candy that she kept in her pocket to nibble on every once in a while.

Tom probably would have forgotten Laurie if it were not for the St Christopher medal he wore, the medal she had given him. Once when he decided to remove it, the chain having become too short, he recalled Laurie's sad, expressive eyes. For a moment they seemed to reproach him so that he bought a new chain and replaced the medal around his neck. When anyone asked him about it, he said it was his lucky medal. He was seventeen now and girls were his preoccupation. They hounded him, and he enjoyed every minute of it.

Laurie was not so lucky, but it happened that she developed a friendship with a British boy who had been watching her play softball. She had joined a girls' team that summer and enjoyed the game.

Her second-hand slacks didn't fit her properly and wouldn't stay rolled up. When she paused after running from base to base she would roll them up again. She was self-conscious about her long skinny legs but they sure ran well. Suddenly, she heard a group of boys chanting from the bleachers, "L-E, L-E, L-E-G-S, roll up those slacks legs!"

At first embarrassed, she soon realized that it was a friendly chanting, led by some of the boys from St Michael's Academy, namely Jack Dowe and the Boyle brothers. They were cheering her on!

When she went in for her break, a boy came forward and said, "Good show!" He had a British accent which never failed to impress Laurie. He struck up a conversation and told her that she looked like Vivian Leigh in *Gone with the Wind*. Now, this could easily be classed as a grade A compliment. She was soon eating out of his hand.

Andrew was gangly and uncoordinated, somewhat of

an outcast like herself, but with a sophisticated accent and impeccable manners. Nevertheless, this did not solve the problem of her need for affection, for Andrew was a perfect gentleman. With some gentle prodding from her brother Murdo, he was told there was a green light ahead with Laurie.

One evening the shy couple took a walk by the river and sat on a boulder to watch the sunset. The mood was perfect and Laurie waited for what seemed like ages, as they manoeuvred their faces close enough without actually appearing to do so. Laurie was as tense as a chain link fence till the kiss finally came. It not only missed her lips, but it sounded like a cow getting out of a swamp. Andrew looked at her and said, "hammy, isn't it?" She said something kind as she wanted to get on with it. They obviously needed lots of practice. But Andrew had done his duty.

Laurie, frustrated in her attempts to gain even a minimum of sexual experience, learned the facts of life bit by bit and very slowly. That year she accidentally learned a bit more.

No, Jamie no, oh please, Jamie, no! Laurie lay in bed and listened and wondered what Mom was on about and then in a flash it hit her. Jamie got up and she heard the sound of a drawer open and close before he returned to bed. She had sneaked a look into the tiny metal box of prophylactics. It contained glass tubes and she couldn't figure out how they worked.

Since Serafina was a Catholic, she wasn't to use any contraception. She already had six babies so she couldn't protest too vigorously for fear of having another. But she must protest, as if by protesting it lessened the gravity of the sin, and perhaps the priest would understand when she next went to confession, for after all her husband was a Protestant.

Laurie felt strangely upset, for now she had positive proof that they actually did do *it*. Till now, she knew they must have at one time because that's how children were made, but she didn't know if it still happened until that morning. She had no word for those things in the little metal box, because having seen them, she quickly shut the lid feeling like a sneak. She felt sorry that she knew and yet secretly glad that they were there.

The box had the word Sheik on it, under a picture of an Arab in full dress. She had seen the silent movie and conjured up visions of being captured by a handsome sultan. He would carry her off to his tent and seduce her into forbidden love. She thought the Arabs must have invented the things because they were so hot-blooded.

It was not until many years later, when she bought a car, that she recognized the tiny glass tubes, the fuses that her dad had stored in the empty prophylactic box and, remembering, smiled.

She had no word for what her mom and dad were doing. The bold girl at school, the one who said "hey, Red" to Sister Henrietta (who had a wisp of red hair showing through her head gear), stopped them – she, Barbara and Cathy – on the stairs and told them that the man put his dick inside the woman and made a baby. Disbelieving and disgusted, they swore that their parents had never done such a thing. But that was several years ago when Laurie was only fourteen and she knew better now, but not much more.

It was futile to be curious. The only books available were the ones in the classroom bookcase, all carefully selected classics and novels. They were allowed one every weekend and she read them all. The only other reading material occasionally available to her were the dime comics, all perfectly bare of even a hint of sex. For some reason she wasn't even curious, for she thought she knew what she needed to know. The words were missing and exactly how was missing, but you couldn't have sex until you were married anyway, because that was the worst possible sin imaginable.

When she was in grade five she found out that babies grew inside their mothers. The girl next door used to taunt their neighbour Mrs Lalonde. When the poor woman passed on the street while in the late stages of pregnancy, Rita would taunt her, "Mrs Lalonde's having a bay-ay bee-ee!"

When Laurie sat down to lunch she came right out and told her dad about it and innocently added, "Mrs Lalonde has a big stomach, maybe she has a tumour."

Serafina took Laurie from the table and in a hushed whisper said, "Babies grow inside their mothers, under their heart."

Laurie's feelings at that moment can only be described in one way. She felt as if she had been hit over the head with a log. She was stunned, felt dizzy and remained silent and stunned for days. Never would she forget the look on her mom's face when she told her, her big anxious eyes and her trembling voice.

But even then, she had no curiosity about how this happened. She was sure, now, that if she had been told how all this was accomplished, she might have passed from shock into something more serious and requiring medical assistance. As it was she sat about unresponsive and robot-like for at least a week.

Serafina had managed to conceal her condition when she was pregnant with Naomi six years ago. She had gone to her mother's place in New York for the last two months with the two youngest, Catherine and Jimmy, leaving Laurie and Murdo with the maid, Edna. But that was when Laurie was seven. Now she was in high school.

Since Laurie had stopped boarding and attended day

school, her situation improved; however, the nuns still plagued her. So out of touch with reality, they made life difficult for any student who did not measure up, namely, one who dressed poorly or who was not impeccably clean, or who did not have funds readily available for their little projects and charities.

It was hard for Laurie to look clean wearing her one and only uniform every day with no money for dry cleaning, harder still to concentrate on school work when she left a home where quarrelling and bitterness was the norm, and when she often returned to an unappetizing meal, cooked and served with indifference and eaten in an unhappy atmosphere.

The nuns were very particular about things that would not have mattered in any other school. The sister who supervised the cloakroom in the basement insisted that they have a cloth bag to put their overshoes in. They were to hang it on a hook so as not to dirty the floor. Serafina didn't sew, nor was there money to buy cloth bags. Laurie was the oldest so she bravely tried to explain to the nun that they couldn't afford them. It was the one time she actually got enough courage to say this, possibly because the nun was a stranger and the other girls had left the room.

The nun shouted in French, which by then Laurie could understand, about how the English could afford chocolates and all manner of luxuries, but pretended to be poor. She probably would have given anything for a chocolate and hated being stationed in that damp basement tunnel to make sure the girls left nothing on the floor beneath their coats. Laurie never saw her smile once during the entire school year.

In the classroom, Laurie was constantly derided for what Sister Henrietta called being in the moon. "What's it like up there, Laurie? Tell us what it's like up there," she said.

That she should assume Laurie was always daydreaming merely because she did not look attentive or because she did not always hear what was said was, to a certain degree, unfair. That she was right once in a while was true, but most of the time that was not the case, for you see, the girl was a very deep thinker.

If what Sister said was intriguing, Laurie would immediately pursue it into her subconscious. On the other hand, if she was incomprehensible, the girl would, of course, become distracted. But she knew that later, when she could read the textbook, it would become clear to her. It was always easier for her to understand the written word.

Hence, when Sister said, "Tell us what it is like up there, Laurie," if she could have dared answer, it would have been to say, "Disturb me if you must, dear Sister, but ridicule me not, for deep thinking is essential to the creative process and I cannot reserve a special time for inspiration."

What the nuns failed to see, all but one, was that Laurie was very tired. She had been working all summer in the Jewish General Hospital and now worked every Saturday at Simpsons' as a salesgirl in order to help her mother.

There was only one classroom sister who did not ridicule Laurie and who understood her situation. This small pretty nun would treat her with the same respect she would give any other adult, for which Laurie was thankful. There was a mystery surrounding this sister, as she seemed, most of the time, to be suffering some sort of martyrdom. Laurie, always the incurable romantic, thought it was a broken heart.

5

Laurie's sixteenth birthday was not the joyous event which she thought it should be, because it came and went without anyone taking any notice whatsoever. That morning she had proudly announced that she was "sweet sixteen." Serafina was shopping in Montreal so Laurie expected her to return with a gift. But when her mother returned, she ignored the girl. Serafina was eating from a small bag of salted peanuts when Laurie confronted her.

"Well?"

"Well what?"

"It's my birthday."

"Oh yes, here, take these." Perplexed, Laurie accepted the little bag, and then, looking into it, wondered if it was all a part of some cruel joke.

There are no words to describe how she felt other than the truth. She detested her mother. She had given her all of her last pay check. "You bitch," she said.

Then, of course, all hell broke loose. "Guess what Laurie called Mommie" rang from room to room. Serafina took full advantage of the situation, playing it for all it was worth.

Laurie had never used such a word before, as it was considered just about the worst thing a person could say, but she had been pushed to her limit. She was a good girl, dutiful and obedient, and she very rarely asked for anything for fear of being a burden. Yet she was treated differently than her brothers and sisters, who were allowed to be carefree and who, although certainly not pampered, did not have to wear second-hand clothing or endure the hardships that she did.

When Jamie came home, he marched her down to the basement and told to take down her panties. When she felt the leather belt bite into her buttocks, she gasped, but this time she refused to cry. After three lashes, she still had not screamed. She turned around and looked at her father with contempt, surprised to see an embarrassed look on his face. He put down the strap and asked her to leave.

Her brothers and sisters, who usually gathered at the top of the stairs, at first with excited anticipation, usually broke into tears after hearing her scream in pain. By the time Jamie finished, at around six to ten lashes, there would be such a cacophony of screaming and crying by all six of them, that it resembled a movie she had seen, where a Christian was thrown to the lions. But this time when she quietly and in a dignified manner walked upstairs, they made way for her and incredulously remarked, "She didn't cry! she only got three."

Serafina was upset when she heard Laurie's screams. She thought Jamie was wielding the strap too heavily. At such times she felt a stirring of guilt, but it didn't last for long. She couldn't fully understand why she demanded that Laurie be punished. The reasons were too complex.

She and Jamie didn't have the kind of companionship that she craved. She thought of how different her life was, when compared to other married couples. They did things together, went to the movies or for walks. Jamie spent all his free time alone hunting or fishing. He never gave her cards or presents, not even at Christmas, and she never got enough household money. He said that he had to pay the bills first because she bought things that they really didn't need. That wasn't fair, she thought, because she always looked for bargains. He was selfish because when he went hunting for a weekend, he took steaks and chocolates, luxuries they never had at home. She never felt she came first in her husband's heart.

Jamie felt justified in beating Laurie because the Bible said if you spared the rod you would spoil the child. That the punishment was too severe for mere sauciness never occurred to him.

He didn't understand why Serafina couldn't get along with Laurie. The girl had a mind of her own and often would not accept no for an answer, asking why not? — never satisfied with a "because I said so." Children had no right to question authority, and his thrashings never did him any harm when he was young. He remembered a poem his mother Lila taught him when he was a boy. It was a poem about table manners.

"I must not ask for this and that and murmur if the meat is fat, I must not say a single word, for children should be seen not heard."

But Laurie was now a young lady. What should he do?

He did not consider it appropriate to thrash a young lady. It was the way she had looked at him with what he called those "come to Jesus eyes." He suddenly realized that if he ever did it again, she would no longer love him. He supposed it was acceptable for someone who was sixteen to have an opinion of her own. By God! he thought, she had some real smart answers too, leaving him lost for words.

As for Serafina, he wasn't getting along with her. They were always arguing. He just couldn't get his point across. If she didn't insist on sending the children to the Catholic schools, he wouldn't have to pay a double school tax. Why should he be penalized for being a Protestant? And they just couldn't afford to give the girls piano, ballet and art lessons. Now she had arranged to have the kitchen remodelled and it was going to take a whole year at least to pay for that. She came home with a new winter coat last week, a bargain, reduced to only eight dollars, she said. When he asked her if she needed a new coat she thought he was being unreasonable. She didn't get the point. Eight dollars could buy a lot of food.

She constantly complained about having six children, as if God had singled her out for some sort of martyrdom, and yet most Catholic women had as many, if not more. What else could she expect if she believed that the Pope's word was law? According to her, she had easy labour and her mother Dolores was a big help. She also had a maid when the children were young, a luxury nearly unheard-of among the people he knew.

Jamie didn't know what to do about her nagging. She was seldom content, even though he nearly always helped with the cooking, something that very few men did.

He recalled how they first met. He was working for the cable company in New York, rented a room at the Micallef house. It was there he heard Serafina play the piano. He would often sit on the stairs listening to her, but dared not approach her because of her brother Joe. Joe didn't want her to marry a Protestant, watched over her like a father. But their mother, Dolores, soon noticed how he felt about Serafina. Luckily she took a liking to him and allowed him to take her out. Joe reluctantly agreed to the marriage when it became obvious that Serafina was in love. But he was concerned about her leaving to settle in Canada. Jamie didn't like New York, not after living in Canso.

Jamie assumed that his wife could cook and keep a house in order, but he soon realized it was Tessie, her sister, who had done the housework. Serafina played the piano for a silent movie theatre, played fast when there was action, like during a fight, and slowly for the romantic or touching parts of the film. Jamie thought it fascinating, the way she could switch from one mood to another. He remembered the fun they had in those days; Serafina must have expected marriage would be just more fun. I guess she never really grew up, he thought.

Now she would use any number of excuses to get out of the house, belonging to several women's organizations for good measure. Once she phoned Jamie's sister, Hazel, and said, "I have a headache, let's go to town," town meaning Montreal, the last place on earth Hazel would want to be if she had a headache. But she understood what Serafina meant.

She loved to dance and would do so at every opportunity with abandon. When people would remark on it, saying, "Where do you get the energy after all the housework?" or "How come you look so young?" or "How do you do it?" she beamed with pleasure.

Once Jamie said, "Why don't you tell them how you do it? Tell them the truth; you sleep till past noon."

That remark had made her angry. She was a night person, staying up till all hours, listening to the radio or reading novels while sucking on hardball candies or peppermints, and when the children came home for lunch she was sound asleep.

The beatings stopped, and the nearest that Laurie could figure out was that it had something to do with her womanhood. She no longer had the body of a child. Perhaps her dad had noticed and felt uncomfortable. It could also be that because it was the first time she didn't cry, he instinctively knew that it was time to stop.

But Laurie's punishment went much further, because they lived in a small town where everyone knew just about everyone else. As she walked down to the village the next day, she met her Aunt Hazel. "I heard what you called your mother. Shame on you," she said.

Because Laurie really loved her aunt, she sought her approval. Once in a while when she visited her, Hazel taught her how to bake something special. They thought alike and everyone said that not only did they look alike, but they talked in the same way. Laurie often wished that her Aunt Hazel was her mother. Serafina had been busy telling everyone what her daughter had said, and by the time Sunday came around Laurie would not have been surprised at all if the priest had announced it from the pulpit. She felt as if the whole town knew, so for a while she tried to avoid meeting anyone.

Jamie was a good-looking man but appearance was not important at all. He would embarrass his family by going around town in torn and dirty clothes that looked as if the dog had slept on them, which he very well may have done. Like the typical outdoors man he was lean, wiry and tanned both summer and winter.

That he spent his vacation time alone hunting and fishing, and took no interest in keeping his home in good repair, was not to his credit. But when his picture appeared in hunting and fishing magazines, alongside his Labrador retriever, with articles about his exploits, his family felt proud of him.

Laurie believed it was wrong to kill for pleasure, but since they needed the fish and game for survival, just as the Indians did, that made it all right. That Jamie derived such pleasure from his sport, she was prepared to forgive, because she realized that part of the pleasure came from a pride in being able to feed his family. He never hunted out of season, never took more than his quota, nor killed anything they did not need for food.

Once, Laurie broached the subject of journalism, understanding, of course, that he couldn't afford to send her to college, priority being given to the boys. She wanted him to know that she had a love for learning, and he said something that flabbergasted her. "There is no need for you to go to high school, dear, because you'll be getting married."

"But Dad," she said, "I've already finished high school."

"Oh, have you dear? That's good." His last remark was a revelation, and although she knew he didn't intend to hurt her, he did.

When Murdo decided he wanted to be Jesuit, Jamie was really upset. He had such dreams for his oldest son and here he was going off to Guelph to do he knew not what. It was the only time Laurie ever saw her father drunk.

He went down to the river with a bottle and a fisherman had to bring him home. Laurie's heart went out to her dad, for how could a Baptist understand his son wanting to be a Jesuit?

As for Laurie, she couldn't understand how a sex maniac could be Jesuit. Murdo, handsome with black hair and dark eyes, was very concerned about his appearance. He looked Maltese and resembled Serafina in some ways. He was crazy about girls and it was with his sister's help that he usually got an introduction to some of the prettiest girls in town. But that was not the reason she thought he shouldn't be a priest.

Murdo, Laurie thought, was obsessed with sex. She discovered nude drawings of women hidden in his schoolbooks. There was no doubt in her mind that they were very erotic. Of course, it was pretty normal for a boy of sixteen to be engrossed with thoughts of sex, but she didn't know that.

Once, when Grandma Lila visited, she decided to turn all the mattresses. She found one of Murdo's drawings under his, and came down to the kitchen with it to show Serafina and Laurie. "Look at this lewd woman with these monstrous breasts, so big that they made me blush," she said, and indeed, her face was still flaming.

Laurie thought Serafina would be shocked and that Murdo was in for it, but to her surprise her mother said, "I didn't know he was such a good artist."

Murdo did leave for Guelph, and although Laurie felt sad, she felt proud too. And her dad felt better when he visited the Seminary for he found it to be a happy place. The men were self-sufficient, even to growing their own food, he said.

And there was always his younger son, Jimmy, who loved sports, and went fishing with his father. He looked like him, even sounded like him on occasion, with one exception. Jimmy was an extrovert, a showman and very social, whereas his dad was a quiet man.

When Catherine entered the convent to become a nun a few years later, Jamie made no fuss at all. After all, he had four girls, so surely he could spare one. But Laurie was very upset, not so much about her sister being a nun, but because she was joining a Quebec order that was mainly French. She knew that Catherine would be lonely. Sure, Catherine would learn how to speak French, but it was not the same as being with a group of American nuns who were more modern and understanding.

Laurie also knew that she would rarely see Catherine, because how could she visit her sister in a place that had such unhappy memories? But she was afraid that if she tried to talk Catherine out of it, and succeeded, she would be guilty of a sin.

Finally, the day came when Catherine was to leave. She was sitting on the sofa with an extremely sad look on her face. Laurie knew instinctively that her sister was having second thoughts, so when Catherine looked up and said, "Suppose there is no God and all this is for nothing," Laurie could hold back her tears no longer and said, "You don't *have* to go!"

Catherine wished that her father would protest her going. Could it be that he didn't love her very much? A friend of hers, who was entering, had parents who fought it till the bitter end. She needed to feel that her mom and dad considered her leaving to be their sacrifice, their loss, albeit God's gain. Tears and protestations would have been very appropriate.

Since it is nearly impossible for a father always to do and say exactly the right thing at the right time, each of his children must have different memories. When Laurie thinks of her dad, she remembers his gentleness when she was sick, his praise of her achievements no matter how small, and his complete honesty. She pictures him in his garden which he loved, talking to Creek, his Labrador retriever, both of them talking to the birds, and she longs for roast duck, the skin all crackly and brown, with his special dry stuffing, so much so that she can almost smell it.

Serafina, no longer able to induce her husband to beat Laurie, became increasingly more critical and demanding. She became so unkind to the girl that it became obvious. She would ridicule her when she tried to sing or play the piano, so Laurie would sing and play badly, deliberately making a joke of it. Serafina's remarks about her were usually negative: "Laurie isn't patient, Laurie isn't sentimental, she's cold, she isn't good with children, she has no figure." But she often said that Laurie was so funny that she should be a comedian. So Laurie tried to make her mother laugh.

Jamie told Serafina that if she did not change her attitude, he feared their daughter would run away from home. He was right, but it wasn't as easy as all that. Where was she to run to? She did start planning her escape, however. She would take the only route open to her and apply for nurse's training, where she would labour for her room and board. But that was months away and till then she must persevere.

It was by chance, when she was much younger, that she had discovered the King James version of the Bible that belonged to Jamie. It was the language that hooked her. How beautiful! she thought...and read on. She had learned Bible stories as a child and had access to a small modernized version of the New Testament in school, but it was only with the King James version that the reading itself gave her pleasure. She took comfort in the ancient words and her Faith sustained her.

When Laurie began dating Bill Ryan, life took on a different meaning. He had been a novitiate at the Jesuit seminary at Guelph with Murdo. They left simultaneously, and later, Murdo introduced Bill to his sister at a Loyola dance. Bill was clean-cut and wholesome looking. Laurie couldn't believe her good fortune.

When he became a paratrooper and showed up at her door in uniform she realized he looked like Prince Philip, who would one day marry the Queen. They had not been dating each other for long, but long enough for Laurie to realize that he would make a wonderful Catholic husband. And long enough for her to think she was falling in love.

She and Bill were of a religious nature and from a similar background, making them well suited. When Bill was invited to have supper at Laurie's, she was very tense about the prospect. Her uncle Don voiced her fears when he said, joking as usual "If he meets this crazy bunch he'll leave you for sure."

But Bill didn't turn a hair. Everyone was on their company behaviour: Murdo with that faraway expression on his face as if he was from a distant planet and only here by some accident of fate, Catherine because she knew how much it meant to Laurie, Jimmy because she had promised him a quarter providing he didn't say anything embarrassing, her little sister Naomi, the only blond in the family, sitting pretty, and Lana the youngest, whom Laurie had mothered so often, as cute as a button, with her round face and smiling dark eyes. Laurie had nicknamed her "Papoose."

When it was Laurie's turn to visit Bill's home for supper, there was a lot of hilarity and banter, but she felt excluded because she didn't know what they were talking about. Happy nonetheless, because she was near Bill, she wondered how his mom got away with having only two children, as opposed to their six, being a Catholic.

Bill was always wise-cracking and he had a very cheerful nature. He didn't wear his religion as a yoke around his neck, didn't talk about it, just lived it. He loved opera and took Laurie to see Pagliacci and Faust.

Thinking at first that she would be listening to a bunch of screech owls, she found herself deeply moved to the point of shedding tears. She developed an appreciation for opera that would stay with her always.

Before they could come to an understanding, and before they had progressed beyond a kiss, Bill went overseas. His letters were few and she feared he had forgotten about her, but she continued to knit him socks and to mail them.

He never came back and she believed he died because he was too good to live. When she thought of Bill Ryan, she pictured him laughing, and she knew he would always to be in her prayer on Remembrance Day.

Not long after, the war ended. It had just been announced on the radio, when Laurie's dad invited her to kneel with him and say a prayer of thanks. They silently prayed together.

Since it seemed at the time that love would always pass her by, Laurie became depressed, and she would cry often. She took to going on long walks alone by the river by way of Tiffin Road. Narrow, unpaved, and lined with magnificent trees that formed a canopy overhead, it was called Lovers' Lane. She felt as if she was in a green cathedral. But church gave her no comfort now. When she watched the spectacular sunsets from the river's edge, they moved her, but only served to deepen her depression.

On one such evening, when the moon lay down a shining silver road upon the water, inviting her to follow, she dipped her oars into its molten path and made straight for Moffatt's Island. She slept and was made whole again, as the stars stared down in silence.

Gypsies camped in the fields nearby for a few weeks every summer. One day as Laurie was picking wild strawberries, she saw a gypsy at a table near her caravan. Surrounded by onlookers, she unwrapped a small glass ball and reverently placed it on the table. Laurie watched the scene in fascination. When about to leave, the gypsy beckoned her, and so she shyly approached.

"Would you like to have your fortune told?" the woman asked.

"I have no money," the girl replied.

"Free for the lady with the sad eyes," she said.

Excited by the turn of events, Laurie longed to have her fortune told. She rushed over and sat down lest the woman change her mind. The gypsy signalled and the others scattered.

"You go to the island—why?" She smiled, her black eyes gleaming. Her camp overlooked the river and she had seen Laurie go there alone.

"Because," Laurie said, "when I'm there, I feel special."

The woman brushed her hair back with long be-ringed fingers, the bracelets on her wrist jingling with every movement. She looked at the girl gravely with knowing eyes, and then she gazed into her ball. Laurie looked with her.

They were silent for so long that she became aware of the heat crickets humming high in the noonday sun. The herb smell of the fields was pungent. She felt as if somehow the whole scenario was unreal, while she waited behind a shimmering haze of sun and heat. When the gypsy finally spoke she startled her.

"You will have a great love. He will come from the sea."

"Will I marry?"

"Perhaps, but you will not marry your great love. You will give much but you are born apart."

"What do you mean?"

"Your heart is hungry and that is why you go to the island. Your heart will always be hungry."

Laurie listened, trying to fathom the meaning of the words; there was a rushing sound in her ears. The laughing of children seemed to come from far off as she thanked her and made her way back home.

That night she dreamed she was on the island. A man came swimming toward her, but as she watched him, he suddenly met her eyes and dove under a wave. The yellow of his hair sprinkled on the water like grains of gold dust, and he had the tail of a fish.

Why must I so lonely be?
What star above is guiding me
to laugh, to sing and smile,
to love for just a while.
I think that on my natal day
my Angel wept as she did say,
"You will give, my child, but you are born apart,
forever a child, with a hungry heart."

6

The years spent in nurses' training were extremely difficult. Exploited, Laurie worked long hours, sometimes as long as ten if she was on the afternoon shift, sitting down only to eat. Added to this was a course of study that kept her confined to her room every evening. Back pain and aching feet became second nature to her.

The hospital was run mainly by nuns who on the whole were a good lot, but one on obstetrics was so unjust as to be mean, and she made Laurie's life miserable for months. The girl discovered that many students simply refused to accept situations like this and managed to have them changed. But conditioned by nuns for so many years, she was completely lacking in defence mechanisms. It never occurred to her that she had a choice. At the convent, the nuns had forced the girls to lower their eyes and say, "thank you Sister" after a scolding, *even* if they were blameless because, they said, it built *character.*

Laurie had two weeks vacation during her second summer of nurses' training and she was sorely in need of a rest. Delighted to receive an invitation from her Grandmother Lila to visit Canso, she begged to go. Lila had offered to pay half the fare if Jamie would pay the rest.

When Jamie saw Laurie's report card, he became concerned because it said that her health was only fair. When he made inquiries, the supervisor told him that it merely meant Laurie had been sick a few times. He wanted the girl to drop out of training because, he said, it was too strenuous for her. But when she begged to stay he decided that two weeks in Canso with fresh sea air and lots of rest was just what she needed.

Serafina now had her heart set on Laurie marrying a doctor and didn't want her to drop out of training. For once, she was in agreement with her husband about Laurie. The girl needed a rest.

Laurie mostly read on the long train ride to Mulgrave and soon cleared her mind from the cares of nursing. She had passed her probation exams and felt as if a ton of bricks had been lifted from her shoulders. It was with anticipation that she boarded the *Owera* to Canso. When the vessel reached open sea and the water became very rough, happy memories came flooding back, memories of Captain Simms and Tommy, of kind friendly faces and sunny days filled with the sounds of the sea. When she recognized a vessel in full sail, looking so beautiful, she waved and whoever it was at the wheel waved back. She wondered if she would see Tom again. He would be a man.

When she arrived at her destination, she felt elated. After spending an appropriate time with her grandmother, she put on her dungarees and a white shirt and set out for the cliffs above the beach. She came back an hour later eyes sparkling, cheeks aglow and feeling like a new person. Over supper she found out that Captain Simms was no longer there, having died two summers before. After Mass the next morning, she picked an armful of wild flowers on the hill behind the church and paid her respects to Muzzie, Captain Simms, and the grandfather she never knew.

As she stood there looking down at the town, she watched some of the parishioners going to the Catholic church, called the "Star of the Sea." Laurie was thinking that it was such a beautiful name, when she thought she saw Tom. It had been nine years, so she couldn't be sure.

Later she asked Lila if it could have been him.

"Yes, dear, it probably was," she said. "He hasn't changed much. He and his mother have a little house on the tickle." Laurie smiled with pleasure. A tickle was a tiny cove on the bay.

Grandma continued, "He's been building a small vessel. From what I hear, he's a good carpenter, but he's been waiting to get into the seaman's union in Halifax. Forget about him, Laurie. He'll be gone soon and be at sea for most of his life. There's to be Regatta and town fair next Saturday. We'll be going and so will just about everyone else in town. You're sure to make friends."

When Laurie arrived at the Regatta with her grandmother that Saturday, she found the people not only down to earth and friendly, but superb cooks as well. The fair grounds smelled of chowder and the sight of so many jams and pies made her mouth water.

"Grandma, please can I have some chowder?"

"But we have a whole picnic basket full of food."

"I know, but how can you smell that and not want some? Please," she begged, "I've never tasted chowder."

"You've never tasted chowder?!" Lila not only bought a bowl for Laurie, but when she watched the ladies dish it out, succumbed and got one for herself. They both cleaned their bowls and agreed that it tasted even better than it smelled. Laurie wished she had some money, surrounded as she was by so many tantalizing foods and handmade goods.

It was that kind of a day when the sun came and went with the clouds, warm, but not too warm because of the sea breeze. The salt air had worked its magic and Laurie felt full of energy and enthusiasm for life. Rosy cheeked, her long black hair dishevelled by the breeze, she couldn't help but respond to the banter that surrounded her.

Suddenly, a commotion took place, as people hurried closer to the cliffs to better view the ships entering the harbour. They came in full sail followed by all manner of small craft, decorated for the occasion with flags and slogans.

"The men have been painting and getting ship shape for weeks," Lila said. Laurie felt an elation that brought her close to tears as she watched the white sails billowing against a background of racing clouds and blue sky.

"I'm so glad I came, Grandma, if for no other reason than to see this. I will never forget it."

"A ship is a breath of romance," Lila said, "that carries us far away."

Laurie laughed. "Why Grandma, you're a romantic, just like me."

Later, while Lila sat on a wicker chair with a group of ladies, Laurie crossed the grounds to watch a competition. The judge was tasting a blueberry pie, his eyes rolling reflectively as he savoured the morsel. A small group of ladies bent forward, expectantly awaiting his momentous decision. As Laurie watched him, she wished herself in his place because she remembered Aunt Lena's blueberry pie. She ran her tongue over her lips. Just then he dropped a morsel onto the table and without thinking, Laurie made a lunge for it and popped it into her mouth. The ladies looked in her direction, and seeing her giggle, smiled at her indulgently. She was looking down into her bag, searching for a handkerchief with sticky fingers, when she heard a laugh so deep and warm that it stirred her.

She smiled as she looked up at Tom, for she knew who it was before he spoke.

"Here, let me help you," he said. He took his handkerchief and dabbed at the tip of Laurie's nose, as he smiled into her eyes. At that moment the sun broke through a cloud. It seemed as though Tom was beamed down to her with the sun, and Laurie felt a joy so profound that for a moment she stopped breathing.

"I never expected to see you again," he said, "and here you are with blueberry pie on your nose. But you must have a whole piece all to yourself." He ignored her protestations and bought two pieces. They sat beneath a large oak and while they ate they talked of their hopes and dreams.

"You're still as thin as a stick of macaroni," he said, "you haven't changed at all."

"Oh Tom! do I still look so thin?"

"Relax, Laurie, you're so pretty that it doesn't matter." But it did matter to Laurie.

Tom, now taller and leaner, was a man, and so attractive that when Laurie saw his lips move in conversation and saw his crooked grin, she imagined what it would be like if he kissed her. If ever a girl was ready and ripe for kissing, it was Laurie. Then she noticed the medal around his neck.

"You're still wearing the medal I gave you," she said.

"Of course," he replied, looking a bit embarrassed, "it's for wearing, isn't it?"

Now a girl dressed in a white tight-fitting sheath and red high-heeled shoes was walking towards them, a look of annoyance on her face. She had bobbed curly blond hair, pouty full lips and large breasts that jutted out like pyramids. Her earrings, her bracelets and her lips were all the same shade of fire engine red. She's ravishing, thought Laurie, like the cover of a glamour magazine.

The girl spoke. "I've been waiting for you for a half an hour, Tom. You said you'd meet me at the entrance. I waited and waited and now I'm all hot." Tom made his apologies and explained how he had met his old friend Laurie and lost track of time.

"Laurie," he said, "I'd like you to meet Patricia Hickson." Laurie smiled with admiration and a touch of envy. She was about to say something complimentary and appropriate even though she had a sinking heart, but the look Patricia gave her was as cold as winter stone.

"Excuse us, Laurie," Tom said, as Patricia took his arm with two of hers in a proprietary manner, "see you around."

"That's all right Tom, I must be getting back to Grandma anyway. Nice to have met you, Patricia."

Laurie wondered why Patricia didn't like her. She has nothing to fear from me, she thought. I couldn't begin to compete with her because she's everything I'm not.

Making her way back to Grandma, she found a shady spot under a tree where they would later on have supper. Laurie spread out the blanket and busied herself, but she became very quiet. As if in tune with her feelings, the sun hid behind a large cloud. Laurie shivered and wrapped her shawl about her. It was an old one from her mom's second-hand box but it was pretty, a blending of red and green wool that made her think of Christmas.

Lila sensed Laurie's despondence. "I saw what happened, Laurie, don't let it get you down. There'll be dancing later on and many young men are bound to seek you out. Why, you'll have a wonderful time, just you wait and see!"

"Why would they ask me to dance, Grandma?"

"Why, because you're lovely, dear, and there aren't many young ladies in Canso." Not many young ladies, is more like it, Laurie thought. A man wants a full-bodied woman, and I don't fit the bill. If I was born in Mother's time, when the flat look was in vogue, I wouldn't have any trouble at all.

But she was neither ugly nor plain, so all hope was not lost. Having read once in a magazine that a woman should smile a lot in order to attract a man's attention, she remembered sitting on the curb, looking up at Jack Dowe, talking and smiling her head off. After he was gone, she looked in the hall mirror and saw a great big piece of spinach on her front tooth. She laughed out loud at the memory.

As the sun lowered in the sky, the tired revellers packed their baskets with leftovers and shook out blankets. Some loaded tables and deck chairs into pickup trucks. After friendly goodbyes, young families headed for home to put the children to bed for the night. Many of the elderly also called it a day. Lila took her leave as well, insisting that Laurie stay.

The younger men unfolded chairs and set them up around the wooden platform that was to serve as a dance floor. This done, they lit some lanterns and hung them from the trees.

A different atmosphere prevailed now, as the ladies came forward in twos or in groups to get the most advantageous seats, those where they were sure to be seen. Some younger ones withdrew to comb and primp amidst giggles of expectation. The ladies' room was not far, just down a path to Phalen Hall, and Laurie made her way there.

A long full-length mirror confronted her when she walked in. She liked her peasant blouse and full dirndl skirt. The drawstring gathering on the low neckline made her look slightly more endowed than she really was, and the skirt had the same effect. That was why she chose it. She reached into her string bag for her compact, applied some makeup and dabbed some Evening in Paris behind her ears and in the hollow of her throat. It was in a pretty blue bottle with a blue tassel that one of her patients had given her as a gift. She put two gypsy-like rings on her ears that complemented her outfit and was about to leave when, as an afterthought, she pulled the blouse lower on her shoulders. When they had been practising giving each other bed baths at the hospital, her teacher had told her she had a lovely clavicle.

She could hear the music playing as she made her way back, and arrived to find a trio in full swing. Some couples were doing the jitterbug. To avoid looking conspicuous, she stood behind a group of elderly chaperons, while she surreptitiously looked over the men. There weren't many and none of them could even come close to Tom in the looks department, but there were plenty of young boys. Tom and Patricia were sitting with a group not far from Laurie and she tried to avoid looking in their direction.

Patricia took the opportunity to look Laurie over. She looks so different, she thought; sort of Spanish with that pink and black skirt, that sexy blouse pulled off her shoulders and those rings in her ears. It does make a difference! With that thick black hair and those sultry looking eyes she reminds me of that gypsy I saw in the movies last week . . . but she's skinny. Anyway, Tom loves me and soon we will get married. Suddenly she felt uneasy.

She and Tom had been going steady for a year now and she had finally got him to propose. She had let him go so far on their last date that he was in a frenzy, and then she said, "As soon as we get married, we can do anything we want." He had agreed and said, yes, they would marry, so why couldn't he do it now. She said that since they were now engaged, he could, but they had to see the priest the very next day. That had been last Monday and tomorrow the first banns were to be announced.

She was upset when Tom hadn't introduced her to Laurie as his fiancée, and they had an argument. Tom said he just forgot because he wasn't used to it yet. They were having a lot of arguments lately but she guessed it was because Tom was frustrated.

Laurie noticed that as the evening progressed more men appeared on the scene and some of them looked older and well groomed. They stood in the background with folded arms looking over the ladies, before approaching them and asking them to dance. Laurie loved to dance and did so whenever she could, even if it was mostly to jitterbug with her girl friends. Tom and Patricia were on the floor now; she thought they made a romantic looking couple. Tom wasn't dressed to kill like Patricia was. He wore rolled-up dungarees, a white long-sleeved sweatshirt, and moccasins without socks. If he was mine, I'd knit him a blue sweater to match his eyes, Laurie thought.

Startled to realize that someone tall and presentable was asking her to dance, she looked up. Soon they were dancing the polka. He was a good dancer and Laurie was light on her feet. He twirled her about the floor. Her hair swung, her earrings swung and her skirt swirled about her. She was breathless when the music stopped and she sat down gratefully.

Tom had noticed Laurie dancing. He was seated at the time and Patricia had gone to the ladies' room. At first attracted by the way Laurie's skirt swirled, he then noticed her legs. By God, she has beautiful legs! he thought. Whoever would have known that one day she would have beautiful legs! Sweet little Laurie was grown up, must be all of eighteen. He suddenly felt protective of her.

Once the men saw Laurie on the floor, they swamped her with offers to dance. Surprised, she enjoyed every minute of the unaccustomed attention.

As the evening wore on, the music changed to the slow and romantic kind. Some couples paired off and clung to each other. Laurie watched Tom and Patricia dancing. Patricia had her arms around his neck and she was looking up into his eyes adoringly. She said something amusing and he threw back his head and laughed. After their dance they left, arms entwined. He would kiss her goodnight, thought Laurie... lucky, lucky Patricia.

Though she had more than her share of dance partners, she had encouraged none of them. An older gentleman, with a strong Scottish brogue, who was her frequent partner, asked if he might take her home. She protested, not having far to go, but he was insistent. "You'll be safe with me," he said," you should'na go home alone." To prove his point he brought Laurie up to an elderly matron. "Mrs Rice, tell Laurie that it's safe to go home with me."

She laughed,"Well Bobbie, they say that a gentleman is merely a wolf with patience; yes, you will be safe with him, young lady." But, as fate would have it, Bob lost out.

Tom appeared out of the shadows and stood before Laurie. "A dance for old times' sake?" he said. He had done his duty by Patricia, who lived not five minutes away. Now he had no intention of letting Laurie walk home alone, nor with any strange man.

The song was "Stardust" and the vocalist gave it everything he had. The fiddle sounded like a violin and the guitarist plucked on his strings as on a harp. It seemed as if they played just for them. Laurie was acutely aware of Tom's arm about her waist, the feel of his hand holding hers, and when she looked into his eyes, what she saw there made her tremble. She couldn't look away for long, as if drawn to a magnet. She felt as light as a feather. When he drew her closer and she felt his breath on her cheek, it seemed the most natural thing in the world that he take her head in his hand and guide it into the crook of his neck. With her eyes closed she remained locked in his arms, her heart beating wildly till the song ended. When she withdrew, he gently pulled her back and claimed her for another. She lost track of time and when they started to play "Good Night Sweetheart," Tom pressed his lips to her ear. When he said, "Sweet Laurie, do you know just how bewitching you are?" she felt as weak as a kitten and feared her legs would crumble beneath her.

And so they walked home the long way, by the cliffs, as they did long ago. Moonlight traced their pathway as they feasted on each other's eyes, stumbled, and stopped to kiss at intervals. They sat on a boulder on the beach and Tom took Laurie into his arms. He pressed her to his heart.

"My sweet little Laurie," he said," you got to me the moment I saw blueberry pie on your nose, such a lovely nose," and he kissed it. His lips strayed to her cheek, to her ear and her neck, and suddenly, it was as if he couldn't get enough of her. She trembled under his touch and when his lips found hers, she abandoned herself with an ardour that had been stored for years.

"Oh Laurie," he said, "I didn't know ... I didn't know about love. This is the way it was meant to feel! My darling, this must be the real thing because I'm so happy! ...I must fix everything...make everything right again."

He guided her onto the sand and gathered her into his arms so he could feel the whole of her body against his. His precious weight was upon her and she could feel the wild beating of their hearts mingle with the sound of the waves. She was his totally if he wanted her because she could refuse him nothing, but he tore himself away.

"Meet me here tomorrow afternoon at three," he said. "Promise me, Laurie my dear heart, that you will be here." She promised, then he walked her to her door above the beach. Never in his life had he found it so hard to part with anyone.

Tom wanted to tell Laurie how much he loved her, but only when he was prepared to ask her to marry him. The first thing in the morning he would see Patricia and call off the wedding. He felt terrible when he thought of Patricia. He had thought he loved her until now. How is a man supposed to know the difference between love and passion unless he experiences both? Not that he didn't feel desire for Laurie. When he saw her legs, he felt it for sure, but somehow it was different. He knew now that he loved her more than he loved himself.

What would he say to Patricia? Damn! why did I have to lose control last Sunday? What did she expect when she got him in such a state? She had unzipped him and took his hard-on into her hands. He would have done anything she asked just to get into her pants. He must speak to Father Jim before Mass, before he read the banns, but in all fairness he must speak to Patricia first.

It was one-thirty in the morning, too late to ring her doorbell. It would upset her parents. He would go there at eight in the morning, they could talk and he could get to church before the nine o'clock mass. The banns must not be read.

Laurie lay awake most of the night, too happy to sleep. Tom loved her! She felt it in every fibre of her being. They would marry! She would have his children, who would look just like him. They would grow old together and she would be the best wife that he could ever hope to have. She would quit her training if he wanted her to, so she could be with him as soon as possible. She would do anything to be near him.

When Tom called at Patricia's house early in the morning, her mother came to the door in her kimono. "Why Tom, what are you doing here at this hour? Pat's not up yet."

"But I must see her at once, Mrs Hickson, it's very important."

"Well, I don't know, just a minute, I'll go see."

Tom sat on the porch swing and waited. No matter how he tried, he could not come up with any kind way to do what he had to do.

Mrs Hickson reappeared and said, "You'll have to wait till she dresses."

Up in her room Patricia had been sitting in bed reading a novel. When informed that Tom was waiting downstairs, she said, "Let him wait." She was miffed because he had taken her home too early last night. He had worked on his sailboat all day so she supposed he was tired. He was in a hurry to finish it because he had found a buyer and would make a handsome profit. She wished he would continue his boatmaking and open his own shop. Everyone said he was a master carpenter when it came to boats, but Tom yearned to go to sea. She secretly hoped that he wouldn't be accepted. Marriage would be more fun if he were home every day.

She finished the chapter she had been reading and took her time getting dressed. I wonder what he wants at this hour, she thought. Probably more of what he got last week, but he's not going to get it so easily. As soon as he sells his boat, he'll get me a ring. I don't want him to think I'm easy.

Tom looked at his watch. It was eight-forty. He panicked. I can't wait. I must get to church, he thought. He left and briskly walked toward the hill. It was a fifteen-minute walk at least, but if he hurried he could speak to Father Tompkins before Mass.

Laurie sat in church below the statue of St Joseph. He was a carpenter like Tom. She began to pray and thanked God for his precious gift of love, for she realized that not everyone was so blessed. She must have done something right. The Mass had been underway for some time now but she could not concentrate on it at all, her thoughts full of Tom.

Now the priest was walking to the pulpit to make his announcements. It was Father Tompkins, champion of the poor, known to everyone as Father Jimmy. She hoped his sermon wouldn't be long for she was beginning to feel sleepy. She couldn't have slept for more than an hour and she hadn't had any breakfast because she particularly wanted to receive Communion this morning, the most wonderful morning of all.

Father Tompkins looked over his spectacles and surveyed his parishioners all dressed in their Sunday best. They were his flock, good and honest people, and he loved them all. There weren't many problems here save that of the ever present demon of poverty. His was not a rich parish and it seemed that whenever he was about to balance his books, he had to help someone in dire need. He wondered if the roof would ever be repaired. He sighed, cleared his throat, and began his announcements.

"The banns of marriage are announced for the third time between Agnes Higgins of the town of Canso and John Murray of Antigonish." Laurie smiled with pleasure. Other people in love she thought. The priest continued. "The banns of marriage are announced for the first time between Patricia Hickson and Thomas Doyle both of the town of Canso. Anyone knowing of any reason why these two parties should not be wed should notify me at . . ."

Father Tomkins stopped speaking because of a commotion near the altar of St Joseph. They were carrying a young lady outside. She had fainted. I wish this business of fasting after midnight could be done away with, he thought. The hill is too steep to climb on an empty stomach, especially on a hot day like this. Not till he saw through the open door that one of his parishioners was driving the lady home did he resume talking.

"Our sermon today is entitled, 'God works in mysterious ways his wonders to perform,' or in more simple terms, 'Things are not always as they seem to be.'"

Tom waited on the beach that afternoon near Lila's house. As he waited, he worried. Having arrived too late, the Mass had started, but afterwards, he spoke to Father and stopped the banns. The priest was angry, so Tom promised to return as soon as possible to explain further. He had to see Patricia. It would be humiliating for poor Pat, but at least the banns would not be read for the eleven-thirty service when most of her friends would be there. Only the older people who were early risers went to church at nine. So far, he had not talked to Patricia, for when he returned to her house she was livid.

"But I had to leave earlier and I *must* talk to you," he said.

She snapped at him. "If what you had to say was so important then you wouldn't have left in the first place. I'll see you after Mass. Daddy's waiting."

Tom looked at her gravely, feeling sorry for her. "I won't be at Mass today, Patricia, and I think we had better talk now."

His words infuriated her and she screamed. "You're not going to Mass to hear our first banns?! Tom Doyle, you can go straight to hell!" She threw her missal at him and it nicked his ear.

He had never realized until that very moment how brash her voice sounded. Suddenly the bright red slash of her mouth disgusted him. He wondered how he could have thought he loved her. He walked away feeling humiliated, while Mr Hickson gave him a disapproving look. The wages of sin, Tom thought, and he felt guilty.

When Laurie didn't arrive and it was three-fifteen, Tom walked up to the house and rang the bell. There was no answer, so he returned to the beach and waited, keeping an eye on the house. He waited till dusk and then he prayed. "Oh God," he said out loud, "please don't let me lose her, for I don't know how I can live without her."

Laurie was so pale and in such a state that she had to tell her grandmother everything. She had insisted on leaving for home immediately and there was no swaying her. Lila accompanied her on the *Owera* crossing to Mulgrave. She had some relations there she had planned to visit for a few days anyway, and she wanted to see Laurie safely installed on the train.

The poor girl had looked so happy only yesterday, Lila thought, and now she looked terrible, her face all swollen. She had finally stopped crying but somehow it was even worse as she appeared void of any emotion at all, as if she were sleepwalking. She wore a hat with a veil, which helped disguise her condition.

The bay was choppy as they pulled out of harbour, the rain a soft drizzle. Lila knew better than to think anything she could say would comfort Laurie. She put her arm around her and looked through the mist till she saw a face from the past as clearly as if it was yesterday. She said, "It's a terrible feeling, isn't it, dear."

Tom made his way up the hill to Patricia's house, head bent forward, his jacket collar pulled up to protect him from the wind. She had finally agreed to speak to him, and he dreaded the confrontation. The past week had been a nightmare. He thought of Laurie constantly, ate little, and slept fitfully. Where was she? he wondered. Out loud he said, "If she doesn't get back soon, I'll go nuts."

Tom climbed the steps, his feet like lead, and rang the bell. It was an unfamiliar Patricia who opened the door. She wore a blue and white gingham dress with a high neck and long sleeves, a matching ribbon in her hair, her face without a trace of makeup. Tom thought she looked pale, delicate and innocent. And completely phoney. What's she up to now? he wondered. At any other time he would have laughed, for it was such a contrast from her clinging sheaths, slitted skirts, low-cut or see-through blouses, her heavily made-up eyes and accentuated lips. In male circles she was often referred to as the de-icer. She invited him in with a meek smile.

"We're alone," she said, as they made their way to the parlour.

Even the room looked different, the shades drawn even though it was daylight outside, giving the room a sombre look that bespoke of hidden meanings. Patricia was playing the part of the sweet young girl who had been seduced, in need of protection from the outside world, a protection that only Tom could give her. They sat, Patricia demurely, knees pressed together, hands folded on her lap, Tom on the edge of his chair across from her.

Patricia was shocked by Tom's appearance. He was unshaven, with dark circles under his eyes, and his clothes looked as if he had slept in them. Before she could say anything, he spoke.

"I guess Father Jim has talked to you by now, Patricia. I tried, but you wouldn't listen. It wouldn't be right to marry you because I don't love you. I thought I did, but I was mistaken. I'm sorry for any pain or embarrassment I may have caused you, and if it will make you feel any better, I'll pass the word around that it was you who broke the engagement."

"That's very kind of you," she whispered. It's the least you can do, she thought. I've already done it myself.

After hearing about his return to the dance, she suspected that Laurie was the cause of all this trouble, but she had not expected Tom to look miserable. He appeared tormented, his eyes full of pain. Good! There's trouble in Paradise, she thought. Maybe there's hope after all, now that I have the trump card. She perked up.

"I think I'm pregnant," she announced in a near whisper. Tom blanched, then felt dizzy. He was living his worst nightmare.

"Are you sure?"

"I'll know in about a week...but what if I am, Tom, what then?"

Tom's eyes looked wild as he struggled with words. "I know I must... take some responsibility...if there is a child ...right now I can't think beyond that. We'll talk again when you're sure."

This was not the kind of reaction that Patricia expected. Where was the concern, the tenderness, the awe, even the affection that she deserved? Tom was leaving, his eyes darting about him. She could see that he was in no condition to discuss anything.

As they reached the door, Tom, seeing tears in her eyes, put his hands on both her shoulders and said, "Try not to worry."

When he was gone, Patricia laid her head against the door as she cried desperately, "You belong to me Tom Doyle! I'll never give you up, never!"

It was another week before Lila returned from Mulgrave, without Laurie. When Tom phoned her, she was cold and businesslike, believing he had taken advantage of Laurie. She told him that Laurie had returned home, and would talk no further. Tom, shaken, didn't know what to think except that Laurie had abandoned him, that what happened between them had meant nothing to her but a pleasant interlude. He must have misjudged her ardour and her innocence. It was foolish to think she loved him. She was so young. How did he fall in love so quickly...unless...it was inside him, simmering all these years? That had to be the answer, because he loved her with a certainty that brushed his soul with pain!

His dreams shattered, he saw no point in inflicting any more pain on Patricia than was necessary. He would take his medicine like a man. Now, he paced up and down in front of Whitman's general store where Patricia worked, glanced at his watch nervously, and then saw her coming through the door. She looked her old self again, wearing a leopard print blouse that exposed generous cleavage, a row of bangles on her arms. She smiled prettily as she ran up to him.

"Oh Tom, I'm so glad to see you, I've missed you so much."

"Let's not talk out here," Tom said, as he took her arm and led her onto the wharf. They sat on some cases. Patricia spoke.

"We're going to have a baby. I've been sick every morning. We'll have to get married, but it's all right, Tom. I love you, and I'm sure you love me. It's just that you were led astray. You were weak, but it's okay, I forgive you. Things can be just as they were before Laurie came along. She's gone anyway."

Tom flinched, hearing his worst fears confirmed. He looked down into the water. Forgive me? he thought, for falling in love? for being weak?...no! I was strong. Laurie's not pregnant.

Out loud, he said only, "Life will never be the same," and then, "I'll go see Father Jimmy. Have you told your parents?"

"No, I thought we'd just get married and they wouldn't have to know."

"Well, I'll phone you in a few hours, and then we can talk to them together."

"O.K.," she said brightly, tossing her curls, and then reaching up to kiss him on the cheek, "bye," she said. Tom heard a tinkling sound, then noticed her ears. She bought new earrings, he thought. At a time like this, she wears bells on her ears!

Father Tompkins said he wasn't sure that marrying Patricia was the answer to the problem at hand because two wrongs didn't make a right. It was even more risky since Tom loved Laurie. He suggested that they give the baby up for adoption.

"I know of a couple who would be ideal," he said, "or Patricia could raise it with her mother's help, that is if she was willing. In that case you must contribute financially. And your contribution would not end there, for you will be a father. I'll go over to the house with you if you like, and talk to the Hicksons. You look like the crucifixion. I suggest you see Doctor Moore and get a sedative."

That night when they confronted the Hicksons with the news of their daughter's pregnancy, and the alternatives to a hasty wedding, they rebelled. Tom welcomed Father Tompkins support, for Mr Hickson looked fit to kill. He insisted that Tom marry his daughter. Mrs Hickson was in agreement, because otherwise, she said, she could never be able to hold her head up in society again.

Tom, numb with disappointment, tried to satisfy everybody. He agreed to marry Patricia quietly in a civil ceremony out of town.

"We will let on that you eloped two weeks ago, because when the baby arrives, everyone will be counting the months," said Mrs Hickson.

Tom was kind to Patricia, feeling responsible not only for her plight, but that of his unborn child. Because he didn't love her, he was determined to be a good husband. Many marriages are not love matches and they succeed, he thought. If I really try, maybe everything will turn out all right in the end.

He believed it until the day Patricia made a blueberry pie. He left the table and fled to the beach. A storm was brewing, and as he sat on the very same rock where he once sat with Laurie, waves came crashing at his feet, spraying salt water in his face. It mingled with the salt of his tears and returned with his heart to the sea.

Meanwhile, Laurie seriously considered becoming a missionary sister, but after observing nuns for so long, she could not see that their way of life made them any better at giving. Rather, she had watched a sweet little sister full of spirit and with a happy disposition, one of her classmates, become cold and dour right before her eyes. Many times a nun would say, "God must be pleased with you because you go to Mass and Communion every morning." She found this to be a patronizing remark and it irritated her. Didn't they do the same thing, she thought, so why not me? Nuns and priests have no monopoly on being spiritual! The truth is, she thought wryly, my religion is a crutch.

Crutch or not, without it she probably would not have been able to endure the pain that haunted her. The final years of nursing were almost unbearable for Laurie. Her heart cried out for Tom as her body cried out for rest. If Tom had known of Laurie's feelings then, nothing could have kept him from her, but they both suffered in ignorance.

Considering Laurie's underweight condition, the number of times she fell ill, and the gruelling course of study that taxed her tired brain after a workload heavy enough for two, it was a wonder her spirit did not break. At every turn fate conspired against her, but not once did she consider quitting. Graduate she did, through sheer determination and a belief that this was her vocation. She loved to nurse and she cared about her patients, sometimes too much, as she could very easily become emotionally involved.

Advised to take at least a month off before starting work, Laurie returned home to recuperate in body and mind.

Part

2

Infatuation

I saw the blue of morning skies
The day I looked into your eyes.
I saw golden flecks and a golden dart
Danced straight way into my heart.
I floundered in pools of blue and gold,
I was freezing hot and burning cold,
At once so strong yet strangely weak,
And I walked away on winged feet.

Oh bluely sparkling, smiling, dancing,
Angry, darting, pouting, lancing,
Shouting, kissing, conquering, bold,
Eyes of blue with flecks of gold.

7

Laurie met Kurt Von Roon when she was nineteen and in her last year of nurses' training. He had been a patient of hers recovering from an appendectomy. An extremely handsome German of aristocratic stock, he had lost everything but his accent. Ten years older than Laurie, and with a worldly wise assertive manner, he fascinated her. He had fled Germany when Hitler had become dictator and went to Holland. From there he came to Canada.

She had always been partial to blond or red hair, probably because her hair was very dark. Kurt was so blond that his hair was almost white and his eyes were a very pale blue. He was a very tall and imposing figure with a face and skin that appeared flawless from any angle, so that people stared when they entered a room. She very seldom saw him as he only phoned her for a date once in a while. More often than not Laurie was just too tired to go out and declined his invitations. But Kurt, not accustomed to rejection, continued to phone her.

Now she accepted his invitations because it was a means to get out of the house and see something of life. He'd take her out to supper or to dances, usually at some hall. They went to museums and he taught her a lot about art.

When she brought him home she was nervous because of his being German. Germans were generally open to suspicion and distrust. One's immediate thought on being introduced was to wonder what he had been up to during the war, which although over was still fresh on everyone's mind. Luckily, her family put him at ease; what they lacked in financial comfort, they made up for with good manners, especially at the dinner table and when guests were present.

Laurie could tell that her dad was a bit more reticent than usual though, and when Serafina asked Kurt how he would like his coffee, he answered in a way that unnerved her.

"As black as sin, as sweet as love, and as hot as hell," he answered with a thick accent and a booming voice that sounded as if he were giving an order.

She came into the kitchen and in a loud whisper said, "What kind of a man did you bring home? You make fun of my accent, now you bring home a man with another accent. Arah!"

Although Serafina was Maltese, her English was very good because she had immigrated at thirteen. She loved to be the centre of attention and soon Kurt had her eating out of his hand with flattery.

At first Laurie regarded Kurt as a mentor and another crutch to help her cope with the business of living, but one day after she had seen him intermittently for more than a year, in a single moment that she would always remember vividly, she became infatuated and fell under his spell. She spontaneously experienced the French kiss with a capital F, and then all manner of necking and petting that left her frustrated, but eager for another session. She graduated, so to speak, into his bed where she removed her clothing with the exception of her underwear. They raised a storm beneath the sheets till he achieved his release, but she didn't even consider intercourse. After all, they were not married and he had not said he loved her. She had presumed too much once and would not do so again. But she knew that things just could not go on as they were.

Kurt, having first been attracted to Laurie by her indifference, became charmed by her naive outlook on life. The women he usually dated were sophisticated and perfectly willing to give him sexual favours. Dating Laurie was like visiting a pure spring of sweet water. He had kept coming back for more. But now the situation had changed. He thought he would slowly initiate her into womanhood, but he was getting nowhere. Usually, he would back away in a situation like this, but for some reason he did not.

That she had suffered a lot he knew, now that she had confided in him, and he didn't want her to suffer on his account. For the first time in his life he felt responsible for someone other than himself.

Laurie was in his arms when he asked her if she was happy, and she burst into tears. She believed she loved him and she could not say so unless he told her first, so great was her fear that it would not be reciprocated. Not knowing the reason for her tears and seeking to comfort her, he told her that he loved her. Overjoyed, she shed copious tears, this time of happiness and relief. He, thinking that she was still miserable, said they would marry.

When he found out later that his admission of love would have been sufficient as a starter he said, "You mean I did not have to propose!" but he was laughing.

Once he had spoken of marriage, he could not understand why they could not consummate their relationship. He kept putting pressure on Laurie, who was indoctrinated with the belief that once a man had intercourse, he would no longer respect you, nor marry you. Her anguish was intense. And what if she got pregnant? Kurt said he had rubbers, but they weren't a hundred percent safe. Nothing was. Birth control, other than the rhythm method, was something she could not consider. Moreover, she didn't want a baby until she had been married at least two years. She had already begun taking her temperature every morning, so she would know her fertile period.

This is what it meant to be a Catholic and it wasn't easy. The way Laurie saw it, if you didn't follow the rules, then you might as well be a Protestant. Her Faith was of more importance to her now than anything else.

As it was, she had to tell all in confession, which by then had become a fiasco. She could no more stop necking and petting than she could stop breathing, so the confessional became her second home. For fear the priest would realize it was the same person who burned a hole in the screened partition week after week, she went to another parish across the bridge, to Point St Charles.

This time she was lucky. She didn't get a lecture on the sin of lust, but in a broad Irish brogue the priest simply said, "My dear girl, 'tis your great love that moves you! Don't worry, enjoy yourself and go in peace."

But something strange occurred just two weeks before the wedding. Kurt and Laurie had parked for their usual necking session and Laurie noticed that Kurt's kisses no longer stirred her. Just a few months ago she felt a thrill every time she looked at him. Where had that feeling of excitement gone? She reasoned the only way she knew how. It must be because they weren't having sex. If the lovemaking was leading up to that, she probably would feel something. Kurt still got excited but he was getting some release. She was not, so this explained everything.

Then she remembered how Tom looked at her and she felt a strange burning pain in her chest. But it was better not to remember, she told herself, for you could not always have what you wanted.

She wanted a normal life with marriage and children and she believed she was lucky to have a second chance. She clung to the idea that sex, the ultimate ecstasy, would solve everything.

Kurt and Laurie were married as soon as possible, for Laurie couldn't bear living at home, and for a young lady to live alone then was to risk the loss of her reputation.

When Laurie walked down the aisle, looking like a picture from a Victorian magazine, the wedding guests fairly hummed with admiration. They didn't know the dress was once a five-dollar bargain, two sizes too large, that her Aunt Hazel had bought. Laurie found a dressmaker who took pity on her, and for a reasonable cost filled in the bodice, arms and neck with lace. On Laurie's head was a matching mantilla and she held a bouquet of lilies in her arms.

When she reached Kurt's side, his eyebrows turned up with surprise. Never had he seen her so lovely. Laurie took Kurt's hand for reassurance. He looks so handsome, she thought, and assured. And so relaxed.

Just an hour before she had been struggling to get into the wedding dress; she put it on backwards, got stuck and couldn't get it off again. Her head inside, arms raised, she couldn't move without risk of tearing something. She felt as if she couldn't breathe and panicked as she stumbled blindly out into the hall, crying for help.

"Where is everybody?"

It was her little sister Lana who rescued her. Laurie finally went downstairs to meet Jamie who waited at the front door.

"You look beautiful," he said, his voice filled with awe.

Laurie was so frazzled that she couldn't even recall the drive to church. The house was in a mess; it was dirty. She had not managed to get enough time off from work to do anything, and Serafina, true to form, hadn't a care in the world beyond how she, herself, would look.

Laurie wanted a very small wedding with only the immediate family, but Serafina insisted on inviting just about everyone she could think of, including many who she knew would find it impossible to attend. Her objective, it seemed, was to put on a show that Jamie would take at least a year to pay for, and get as many wedding gifts as possible.

The invitations were late and the reception locale changed at the last minute due to a visit from an acquaintance of Serafina's, a Mrs Pickel, who was reputed to be a warhorse. She literally took over.

"Why not have the reception here at home," she said, "and save a lot of money. The Catholic Woman's League will do the work and all the cooking. Get rid of this and that," she said, pointing to a box full of empty bottles and a pile of fishing equipment, "hide the vacuum, and presto chango! you have a reception."

Laurie panicked. "No," she said, "the invitations are already out, and the hotel will take care of everything."

"Nonsense," said Mrs Pickel.

"Ungrateful," said Serafina, ignoring Laurie.

Now, as she and Kurt kneeled for the celebration of Mass, Laurie tried to unwind. "Well, at least nothing can go wrong here," Laurie thought. But she was wrong.

Mass being over, the priest began the beautiful celebration of Matrimony. Having assured everyone that he could speak English, he blatantly fractured the ceremony, and in his efforts to sound modern, made flippant and inappropriate remarks. Maybe nobody noticed, Laurie thought, but then the soloist, one of Kurt's friends, cracked a note as he sang the Ave Maria. Laurie, already dreading the prospect of the reception, wished the floor would open up and swallow her.

Kurt was in a daze, unaware that anything was amiss. When asked to repeat the words that would make Laurie his wife, his voice quavered and when he tried to put the ring on her finger, his hands shook.

Why, he's afraid, Laurie realized, and at that moment when she looked into his eyes and saw the young boy in him, a sweet tenderness engulfed her. In his weakness she found her strength. She squeezed his hand reassuringly, and suddenly her concerns seemed trite and insignificant, her heart light and filled with peace. When she whispered, "I do," she believed they would be together always.

The Catholic Women's League had done a wonderful job with the reception. It must have taken a regiment of women to transform the place. The food was all home-made and delicious. Laurie felt a tremendous relief, but at the same time resented Serafina and her commandant for having caused her such tension on what should have been the happiest day of her life.

The car Jamie loaned Kurt for the honeymoon broke down, so they headed for the nearest garage. While Laurie sat in the front seat of the car, wearing her gold toned going away suit, gold straw hat with brown and green leaves, her corsage wilting, she felt humiliated.

They know, she thought, as the mechanics worked on the car: they know what we will be doing in a while and that's why they're smiling and smirking. And Kurt is enjoying every minute of it, playing the big stud; doesn't have any idea of what I'm going through.

The car couldn't be fixed, and after a long hot bus ride, Kurt and Laurie arrived at the mountain hotel to discover they were the only guests. They didn't mind, thinking they would be too busy enjoying each other's bodies to care.

Laurie expected the sexual act to be an earth shattering experience, and looked forward to it with anticipation. She loved the intimacy, loved to give Kurt pleasure, but shouldn't there be something for her? She felt nothing save pain at first and then a feeling that some mysterious force, always near and yet beyond her grasp, evaded her. After a week, she assumed that what she had read about woman's pleasure was fiction, and couldn't understand why women were so eager to get married.

At the nearest opportunity, Laurie went to confession and told the priest that she wasn't happy. "I have a feeling that something is missing," she said. "I'm not exactly unhappy, but I feel let down." He didn't understand what she was talking about.

"My dear girl," he said, "you're newly married, you should be on top of the world."

Nothing, not even the marriage preparation course that she had taken at the hospital, suggested the possibility of this, her plight. The priest who had given the course said that the purpose of sexual pleasure was meant to make the hardships of marriage easier to bear. She felt betrayed. Kurt never knew how she felt, as she didn't want to hurt him, and if he had any inkling that she was missing out on anything, he didn't mention it.

On the other hand, Laurie was prepared for their poor financial condition, indeed expected it. They lived in a furnished room which consisted of a bed, a chest of drawers, and a small round table with two chairs that they placed before the window. They shared the kitchen which was downstairs, and a common bathroom, with the other roomers. Kurt had made the living arrangements on his own, and though Laurie was shocked to see where they would live, she said nothing, assuming it was all he could afford. She discovered afterwards, however, that he had simply not made much of an effort to find anything else, assuming it was good enough as a temporary measure. He also had very strict rules about money. Everything was to be salted away for their future home. She couldn't spend any money to make their room attractive, nor could she buy any clothing without his permission, and only if they had a specific function to attend, where his friends or co-workers would see her.

They were to attend a dinner party given by Kurt's employer. Kurt was an assistant manager for a small marketing company but was determined to get a promotion. "I want you to look stunning," he said to Laurie, "not merely pretty, but stunning."

He chose her outfit with care, a black sleeveless wool sheath with tiny velvet braid trim and a small matching cocktail jacket with black velvet collar and cuffs. He accessorized the outfit with delicate silver dangling earrings from Spain. The shoes were black with silver ornament. He took her to a hair dresser that he knew, and had her long black hair done with soft waves, undulating over her ears towards the back, into a sophisticated chignon.

That evening, with his hands on her shoulders he turned her towards the mirror; they both looked at the finished product. Laurie was thrilled, not only about her transformation, but because together they looked like a very romantic picture of a royal couple.

"How did you know that black would suit me?" she said.

"I have an eye for these things. Ideally, emerald green is the colour to complement your eyes, but tonight I want you to look sexy, your skin to look whiter and your eyes more sultry."

And then he said, "Tonight is very important, be nice to Mr Hanlon. When the time comes to consider me for a promotion it will not hurt if he will remember you."

When Kurt introduced Laurie to Mr Hanlon, the man took her hand. He said, "Well Kurt, what have you been hiding?"

Pleased but feeling shy, she said, "How do you do, you have a lovely home."

He put his other hand over hers, holding it captive. He looked into her eyes as he said, "yes, oh *my* yes." Laurie felt uneasy and looked to Kurt, but instead of coming to her rescue he said something that embarrassed her terribly.

"Now you know why I look so tired when I come to work in the morning. Ha! ha!"

Luckily, someone else was waiting for an introduction and she escaped to the powder room to regain her composure.

When she returned to Kurt's side, she said angrily, "How could you?"

Instead of answering he said happily, "You are a hit, my dear, but remove your jacket."

"But I'm chilly."

"I *said* remove the jacket."

He proceeded to remove it himself, smiling as he hissed between his teeth. "I paid a lot for this dress and I want you to look sexy, so do not spoil it."

What could have been a nice party turned out to be a very tense experience for Laurie. Mr Hanlon made sure she sat at the head of the table on his right and during dinner he positively leered at her through slitted puffy eyes, and touched her arm whenever he got a chance. His hand felt clammy, and it was all she could do to nibble at her food as he bombarded her with questions. She could see Kurt had a group of women enthralled by his charms, but he kept an eye on her nonetheless, as if to warn her not to disappoint him.

Mr Hanlon was speaking again. "Please call me Oscar,

my dear. So you like books, eh. Well, I have some first editions in the library. I'll show them to you after dinner." Later she tried to get lost among the guests, but he sought her out, and guided her by the arm into the library.

"Perhaps another time, Mr Hanlon, I haven't met some of your other guests."

"Time enough later." To her consternation he shut the door. They were in a truly beautiful room, its shelves lined with leather-bound volumes. She couldn't help but feel excited by so many, and in such a setting! He showed her a few of his first editions, then he guided her to an alcove where he removed a key from a small ornate box. He opened a glass case and handed her a book. "Something very special I bought in India."

She opened it eagerly, wondering what treasure it held. Her eyes fell upon a very explicit drawing of naked bodies entwined in group sexual activity. She felt herself blush, quickly turned the page, then another, shocked to realize that the book was filled with obscenities. She slammed it shut and hastily gave it to him.

"I don't like it. Let's get back to the party." He came closer and cornered her in the alcove. He whispered through thick flabby lips.

"Pretending you don't like it, eh, but you *all* like it, heh heh." She felt his hand caress her buttock. She pushed him aside and ran, leaving him laughing behind her.

"Yes, you all like it, heh heh heh!"

She insisted Kurt take her home immediately and once in the car he became angry. "What the devil is wrong with you?" he said.

"Your boss made a pass at me."

He smiled. "What did he do?"

"Kurt, you should be angry! He put his hand on my bum."

"Oh my dear girl, you have such a small-town mentality. He probably had too much to drink. Forget it."

"But Kurt, he showed me dirty pictures. I never saw such obscene pictures before. I feel as if I have to go to confession, just because I looked at them."

"You what?" He burst out laughing, and intermittently all the way home he would say "to confession," and then laugh some more.

"I'll never go anywhere near that man, ever again," she said.

Kurt knew that when it came to what she considered right and wrong, there was no swaying her. That he was not outraged at what she considered a personal violation hurt her deeply, but he assured her that he loved her, one of the reasons being that she was so naive.

Thankfully, she no longer had to worry about Mr Hanlon, as he had a heart attack. He probably had it while looking at his book, and playing with himself, she thought. Poetic Justice!

The Blessed Event

Oh to be crucified but once and have it done with!
To suffer the thirsty painful walk to Calvary,
Would it be less than all the sleepless nights
And all the wretched days?
And to have the nails hammered into my hands,
Would it be less than the pain of childbirth?
"Oh Father let this cup pass from me.
Into Thy hands I commend my Spirit."
I say, "release me, damn!, or let me die!"
And my spirit soars, for behold!
My infant resurrection!

8

Laurie successfully used the rhythm method of contraception, the only one permitted by the Catholic church, to delay her first pregnancy. After a year, she and Kurt were both delighted at the prospect of having a child. Laurie hoped that having a baby would pave the way for something better, whatever it was, but again her body betrayed her.

She had expected there might be some morning sickness, but no one had prepared her for the possibility that she would be nauseated and vomiting day and night. She became a shadow of her former self, little more than a hundred pounds and five feet seven and a half inches tall. She couldn't understand why women got married and had babies. Marriage seemed only to benefit a man. Many times in a spasm of retching, she wished herself dead.

But around the fifth month, the nausea eased off and she ate voraciously. Never in her life had food tasted better. By the ninth month she had gained fifty-four pounds and she looked wonderful. Her breasts developed and for the first time in her life she filled a bra.

Laurie felt happy and optimistic. Consequently, when

told there was a complication, that the baby was transverse, she felt jinxed in some way. She went through a long and difficult labour, ending in a forceps delivery, a labour so painful that she was administered heroin.

Laurie felt a tremendous fulfilment with the birth of her first son and happy beyond her wildest dreams. He was beautiful; she named him after St Michael the Archangel, a splendid statue of a handsome warrior angel that graced the hall of the convent that she had once attended.

But her happiness was short-lived. A few days after discharge from the hospital, she was shocked one morning to see a large ghastly looking blue boil on Michael's wrist. It had appeared overnight. She rushed to the Montreal Children's Hospital by taxi and within a half-hour, the doctor informed her that the baby had osteomyelitis, a serious bone infection, usually chronic, and with a very poor prognosis. They had to operate immediately.

First however, they needed her husband's authorization to give an anaesthetic. Kurt was on a business trip out of town and all efforts to contact him were to no avail. Though they gave Michael some morphine, it was less than effective. Laurie stood outside the door of the surgery and wept in torment as she listened to his screams of pain. Afterwards, when she saw his sweet face, now as white as the sheet on the crib, she cried to God in anguish.

As she wept, she implored Him to take anything he wanted from her in exchange for her son's life and health. She laid her hand firmly but gently upon the infant's chest, closed her eyes and willed God to take the strength from her body and give it to her son. She willed with every fibre of her love.

A pure energy came to her from a source outside of herself. It entered her body as a swift current and tingled her fingers as it left. It happened a few times and each time she became weaker. At last, exhausted, she slumped forward on the bed. She tried to rise but her legs would not hold her.

Miraculously, the infection never recurred. But not for a moment did she think herself to be responsible. She was merely an instrument in a process that she could only hope to understand in another life, if indeed another life existed.

Two years later, as planned, Laurie presented Kurt with a new son. It took longer to name her second boy for she was undecided, until one day, while holding her son and listening to the radio, she heard the "Londonderry Air." Deeply moved, she sang to her "Danny boy."

Since she had suffered an equally difficult pregnancy fraught with complications, and because their budget was stretched to the limit, she and Kurt decided that their family was now complete.

But the rhythm method of birth control failed her when she needed it most. The pregnancy made her breathing difficult due to a weak heart valve and she had to take medication. The doctor had advised her not to have any more children, but she had no choice now. Abortion was a criminal offence and she doubted very much if she could have gone through with one in any case, being so Catholic.

Kurt resented this unplanned pregnancy. Laurie couldn't help but recall something he had said when he gave her the engagement ring.

"Of course, you realize that if you do not give me a son, I would be obliged to divorce you. I am the last son in our line." He had a coat of arms ring and each of their sons was to have one. His crest was above the fireplace. Family meant everything to him. Now, it appeared that Kurt was getting more sons than he had bargained for. They named their new son Richard. Laurie sought to please Kurt; it was his father's name.

By the time Laurie's daughter Linda was born, she

realized that the Catholic method of birth control was nothing more than Vatican roulette. Her health was obviously deteriorating. When she was in the hospital after delivery, the priest was making rounds and she said, "Don't come near me."

"What's wrong, my child? " he replied.

"I'm more afraid of having another baby than I am of going to hell."

"Tell me about it."

She poured out her story, not only the problems that she had with her health, but their frugal way of life, how they had never had a vacation, and how hard she had laboured without any help from anyone. She left out nothing.

"You have done more than your share," said the priest, "and since your husband believes there is nothing wrong with birth control, let him use it."

"But Father, when I went to confession before getting pregnant, the priest told me to refuse my husband intercourse if necessary and that things weren't as bad as all that."

"You should have told him to get married himself and find out just how hard it was."

She couldn't begin to express the sublime relief she felt and the admiration she had for this wonderful priest, but oddly enough, her Faith began to change. She realized she could think for herself, that she need not have suffered so much. Her religion had been a rock, but she had been trapped under it.

9

Laurie felt she should be happy. Five years of marriage had brought her four lovely children, a promotion for Kurt, and a new home. Often she would pause to admire it: the elegance of the bay window and white clapboard above red brick, the black door. It was built in the Vermont tradition on what was once an orchard. Apple trees abounded in St Lambert, and their back garden contained three.

Inside, a fieldstone fireplace dominated the sunken living room and a chandelier the slightly higher dining area, both rooms enhanced by ceiling beams that bespoke of colonial times. Wood panelling in both rooms glowed a cherrywood pink in the soft glow of evening light. Their first new furniture, all rock maple, looked warm and inviting. I should be happy, Laurie thought, I want to be happy. Please God, make me happy!

But there were too many dark corners in her life. She felt unloved and worthless in Kurt's eyes, while he acted smug, particularly now that he was a property owner. The house was in his name and it hurt Laurie that he wanted it that way.

To those who knew them, they were a model couple. But underneath the semblance of normalcy a malignancy had taken root. Though Kurt loved his children, he resented Laurie for having them. He often said his life would be so much easier and more peaceful if there were only two. This hurt Laurie, for she could not imagine life without her four children. Each was a gift from God, Linda a special bonus, a reward for stretching her Faith to its limits.

Kurt referred to Laurie as a Catholic animal, good only for breeding children. He refused to become involved with their care and sometimes treated them badly. If one of them cried or annoyed him, he would always use the same words, directed at Laurie: "Ding-a-ling, long live the Pope! You are the good Catholic so you handle it." The bells mimicked those heard during the Mass. Soon Laurie was to dream that she heard them and wake up in a sweat.

Sometimes when the children were sick, she was up all night, but it was pointless to ask for help. If she dared interrupt Kurt's sleep, he would retaliate with remarks that hurt her deeply.

Laurie wondered why Kurt lost his interest in sex. They only made love every few months, but it bothered her more than it bothered him. She felt unattractive. The last time she reached out to him in bed, he had said, "Oh no! I'm tired, I can only give you five minutes." Not that he gave her much more than five minutes anyway. Deeply hurt, she cried herself to sleep, quietly though, because if he heard her, he would consider it a confrontation and become angry.

Laurie wanted to be hugged and kissed, cuddled and cherished, wanted to hear Kurt say how glad he was that he married her and what a good wife she was. Their marriage deteriorated and it seemed to Laurie that Kurt wasn't even aware of it. They never did anything together and they had only been out about three times in the past year.

The last time they had gone out had been for their anniversary. They had plans to have dinner and then go dancing. They arrived at a restaurant to find that a television was on so the customers could watch the football game. Delighted, Kurt sat down, but Laurie protested.

"It's our anniversary. Surely we're not watching the game during supper," she said.

They left, but Kurt was furious and berated her till she was in tears. The evening was ruined, and she no longer cared to go dancing.

And they were always fighting over Serafina. Kurt always took her side against Laurie, "for the sake of peace," he said. But there was no peace inside Laurie, rather an open wound that would not heal. He ridiculed Serafina behind her back but flattered her in public so that she adored him.

One day Kurt stood by the kitchen window with his hands in his pockets. It was Saturday and he was unshaven. Laurie hadn't been able to get him to shower regularly for several years and he often had foul breath. She looked at him and she said to herself, I don't love him any more. Shocked by her own thoughts, she replied, What a terrible thing to think about your husband. It must be that time of the month. You'll feel differently to-morrow. But the feeling of affection never came back.

About a month later she confided in him, hoping for some reassurance, and because she wanted to love him.

"What do you expect?" he said. "People don't still love each other after they have been married for a long time."

Her heart sank. She was hoping for those special words that would rekindle her love and instead she heard a death knell, the sudden realization that his love had died long before hers. When? Did it happen gradually? This last year had been different. They argued at length, accomplishing nothing, and each time she was left frustrated and angry, while he felt cleansed and satisfied.

She was now trapped in a loveless marriage, trapped because the idea of a divorce had not even entered her mind. That was to come later.

When Laurie told Kurt that she feared she no longer loved him, he felt let down, but in no way would he admit it. True, he didn't feel the same about her as he did at one time, but he had always taken it for granted that she loved him. She was his wife, he thought, and who could you take for granted if not your wife?

He hated to see her so tired and he resented a church that could place her in such a position. Although he was Catholic, it was just something he was born into. Why must she take it so seriously?

He also resented her for not enjoying sex more. She got so little out of it that he wondered why she still wanted it. These days, he thought of work night and day. He felt under so much pressure that there just wasn't any energy left for sex. Nothing was so overestimated as sex anyway, he thought.

10

It was the climax of Spring in St Lambert, an afternoon when, at the touch of a rising breeze, apple blossom floated in a frail pink drizzle, to settle on head and shoulders. Laurie, restless to distraction, not understanding the turmoil she felt, started out for Moffatt's Island, but instead she found herself driving across Victoria Bridge, going she knew not where. "If only I could go on forever," she thought. She turned onto the port of Montreal, parked and then found a bench with a view. She was rarely without her children, but today, overcome with a longing for solitude, had asked her sister Naomi to babysit.

Laurie wore a simple dress of emerald green and sandals on her feet. As the breeze ruffled her hair she lifted her face to the sun and closed her eyes. She was attracted by the dockside activity, the calling and shouting, and now the dropping of an anchor as a steamer settled into its berth. She watched with interest as the crew disembarked, boisterous with anticipation, swaggering, not yet accustomed to the ground beneath their feet.

Suddenly a young woman ran out from behind some packing cases into the arms of one of the seamen. They clung to each other and kissed with abandon. Laurie watched, somehow sharing their happiness, but as she watched they became absorbed in a kiss like nothing she had seen before. She shifted in her seat feeling like an intruder as the kiss became more profound, and she felt a stirring and a longing, so that she wished herself in the woman's place. Acutely aware of the seaman's lean hard body, his tallness, she felt his need as if it were her own. A sudden sadness overcame her, and she tried to fight the tears that came unbidden. She looked down and surreptitiously dabbed at her eyes with her scarf. When she raised her head the crew had scattered and the couple had gone.

I must get back, she thought, but still she lingered, trying to understand what had occurred. Another seaman, a straggler, came down the gangplank and walked in her direction. Something about him pulled her, like an imprinting on her soul, and when he was a few feet away she said in a voice that she hardly recognized as her own, "Tom? Tom Doyle!" He stopped in his path and looked down at her. He swung his duffle bag off his shoulder, removed his blue wool toque and stared as if struggling with a memory. He beamed with the same crooked smile and then spoke.

"I remembered your eyes, but how was I to know that you would turn out so beautiful."

She smiled, thinking he had been too long at sea. "So you became a sailor just like you said you would." He sat beside her and told her that his home base was still in Canso, that he was divorced and determined to remain married to the sea. He invited her aboard, and she ceased to care about the time, ceased to care about anything except his eyes, his smile, and his voice.

He was tall, lean and hard muscled, with rugged good

looks, his nose imperfect, looking as if it had been broken in a fight. They stood on deck and looked out towards Moffatt's Island. Laurie told him of her love for the island.

"I can understand why you like it," Tom said. "It looks so wild and isolated because of the rapids, and yet so inviting, sort of a challenge."

Tom could hold back no longer. "I wanted to see you five years ago when I docked in Montreal, Laurie, but when I phoned your home, your mother said you had married. There was so much to explain, but I didn't want to risk upsetting you. Since you were no doubt happy, I also thought it better not to inflict any more pain on myself."

"What is there to say, Tom? You loved Patricia and you married her. You were probably carried away with the mood of the moment that night and then regretted it. It could happen to anyone. But if there is more to tell, then tell it, as I have always believed you didn't intend to hurt me."

So he told her everything and when he said, "I loved you then, Laurie, and I still do," she knew it was the truth.

"Poor Tom," she said, "you have suffered too." They talked of their innermost feelings and it happened so easily, that as the sun gradually lowered in the sky, they felt they had known each other all of their lives.

When she told him of her four children he was incredulous. "How can you have four children, you don't even look married?" She laughed at the funny remark and he laughed with her. "I meant you look so young yourself," he said, and his face became very grave. He held her shoulders firmly and looked deep into her eyes.

"Children yes," he said, "but married no, not really. Your eyes give you away. They are so sad, shy and unsophisticated, the eyes of a girl." She felt herself colouring and couldn't match his gaze.

"You know," she gasped, and trembling, looked away.

It was then she knew for certain that whatever it was that her hungry heart wanted all these years could only be found in him and with him, and so she would remain incomplete for the rest of her life.

Then, simply and spontaneously, she said, "Yes, I love you, but we must never see each other again."

"I agree," he replied. "I can't come between a man and his wife and most of all those innocent children. Nevertheless, you will always be a part of me, Laurie, just like the humming of the engine that I love to feel beneath my feet." When he gathered her into his arms and kissed her it was a confirmation of his love.

"Please pray for me," she said.

"I haven't prayed for years and my past is nothing you would admire. I have done some things that would make your hair curl. But I'll learn to pray again for you. Your eyes are like stained glass windows and it will be as if I'm in church when I remember this day. Yes, Laurie, prayer will come easy again because of you."

Dazed and shaken, she felt his kiss like an indelible mark on her lips. She resolved that what had happened was a gift of sustenance, that somehow it would make life more bearable. Now she must be a wife and a mother, for that was the reality of life, that was her duty.

But duty, much more noble than love, weighed heavily on her shoulders.

One day blended in with another and she was determined that no one should know of her secret. She plunged into the usual round of work with a vengeance. The house looked like a picture from a magazine. As she surveyed her work with satisfaction, it suddenly occurred to her that although the house always looked clean and welcoming, Kurt had remarked on it only once. She remembered the incident vividly because it had given her such pleasure.

He had come home from one of his business trips and while he removed his coat, he said, "It's so good to come home to a clean house. I visited friends while I was away and their place was filthy."

And yet there was no limit to the amount of work that was expected of her. Kurt had a chronic stomach ulcer since long before they met, but cigarette smoking had made it worse. Now his doctor told Laurie that she must prepare special meals for him. It was difficult and time-consuming. She knew that when Kurt stopped smoking the pain disappeared. "If I had any gumption," she thought, "I would tell the doctor that Kurt deserves to have an ulcer if he insists on smoking."

Not only did she cook special meals, but she served them after the children had eaten, because Kurt said they made him nervous.

Because Kurt no longer desired her and resented her so much, she felt herself lacking as a wife, but she knew she was an exemplary mother. Her own childhood had given her valuable lessons on what *not* to do. But the truth was, she enjoyed her children so much that she couldn't think of anything she would rather do than be with them. The developing child's mind fascinated and delighted her.

One day as she was doing the dishes, she looked out of the kitchen window and saw Danny and Richard waving to her from the apple tree. Their sweet smiling faces, filled with the joy of living, moved her deeply and overcame her with sadness. Had she ever been so happy? She must have been at some time. Leaving the dishes to soak, she took up her pen. The poetry she wrote in the days to come was about her children and it was to be her salvation.

Reflections on an Apple Tree

I look from my window and I see
Danny and Richard in the apple tree.
I smile and wave, for I know too
how the sky is heady and the apples sweet.
Oh! how I wish I were high in that tree
where my reflection, my love, grins down at me.

11

It was February, and under a dull and blustering sky, Laurie faced the challenge that came with winter. Michael and Danny were in school and the youngest were having their afternoon nap. The house was silent except for the strident whine of the wind against the windowpanes. It was an eerie, depressing sound. Laurie lost track of time as she watched the blowing snow in a state of semi-awareness.

When she came out of it, nearly a half hour had passed. The sound of the mailman had interrupted her trance and she slowly went to the door. An envelope was addressed to her in a hand that appeared vaguely familiar. The post mark was from Australia. She tore it open, her heart beating wildly. It was a valentine, and though unsigned, it wrought a change in her so fundamental that it defied all reason.

There occurred in her an awakening so intense that she found herself imagining raw sexual encounters with Tom aboard his ship, encounters so earthy that they rang a bell of warning in her brain, and she felt sinful. If her thoughts were only such as these, she could have overcome them in time. However, desire was only one side of the coin; the other side was far more significant, for it seemed that all the powers of the universe bid for her soul.

For suddenly her world was transformed. She became aware of sound and colour long forgotten. During the worst of winter, she no longer felt the cold, but walked with thoughts of Tom, mittenless, open necked and singing. On the long snowy path to the village behind her home, she could shed her mask of propriety and abandon herself to feeling.

Come Spring, she took deep breaths to savour the smell of grass and herbs and she stopped to look at flowers. She recalled all the poetry that she loved so much and recited as she walked. It was as if all the moments of elation that she had ever experienced in her lifetime had condensed and come back to her.

Music took on a new significance and she began to play records of classical music, pausing in her work to wonder why she had never noticed how hauntingly lovely was a melody. The Bible says, "Eye hath not seen, nor ear heard, nor has it even entered into the heart of man, what God hath in store for those who love Him." Well, she came very close, as close as one can get, because she loved so much that she found God.

But it was the change in her appearance that concerned her. She was her own worst critic, but for the first time in her life, when she looked in the mirror, she admitted that she looked pretty good…and much too happy.

Her eyes, usually multicoloured, with their predominant colour difficult to ascertain and changing, depending on what she wore, were now a clear luminescent green. She looked so different that people remarked on it and she feared that her secret would be known.

And yet, for every euphoric hour she experienced, came two of suffering. In a sense she was living on the threshold of a dream world. All sensations were open to her but one. She could not experience love in full measure. The door had been opened to her but she could not enter.

When I am old and children ask about love,
as children often do, I will remember:
The snow as it lay all gleaming
catching crystal from the trees.
I ran heedless with the clouds,
went singing into storms,
walked warm and happy with my heart,
and nightly smiled my dreams to sleep.
I felt as new as Springtime
with a banner upon my sleeve
and I was never before so lovely,
so I feared the world could see
tears that welled too quickly
and left a haze upon the moon,
when the red gold darts of Autumn
seared me with their fire.
Now a sigh unbidden comes,
tears turn and hide under laughter,
and I am born again with painful joy,
when children ask about love
as children often do.

12

Whereas Kurt took no notice of Laurie when she was unhappy, he now became aware of a change in her. He saw her smiling to herself.

"What the hell's the matter with you," he said.

"Nothing, I'm fine."

"Too fine if you ask me. You're up to something."

He watched her like a hawk, so that she became afraid to even *look* happy when he was around.

One day she came in to find her bureau drawers emptied, their contents scattered. Kurt grabbed her by the arm, dragged her into the bedroom, and shut the door.

"What's this?" he said, as he brandished the envelope in her face. "I want the truth."

Not wanting to hurt him, she said, "It's just a valentine from an unknown admirer."

Infuriated, he struck her. She fell back against the wall, terrified. He grabbed her shoulders and shook her till she said, in a quavering voice, "The truth, yes, the truth. I fell in love. I didn't ask for it, but it happened."

Oddly enough Kurt calmed down. He stood over her, his arms folded. "Are you having an affair?"

"No, I never see him and I never will."

"Who is he?"

"What does it matter?"

"What you need is an affair. Tell this man that you have your husband's permission to see him. Once you get this out of your system, you will probably feel better. But I must know who he is because I must approve of the man. He may phone me if he wishes and get my permission personally. An affair is the civilized way to do this. It is the way it is done in Europe."

"I could never do that, I'm not sophisticated enough. It's dishonest and if the children found out they would lose respect for me. Anyway, he's gone. We agreed never to see each other, so please forget it. I was not unfaithful to you."

"Does he love you?"

She tried not to hurt him; "I don't know."

In a steely voice he said, "So he's just someone sniffing around for some action and you've been parading in the gutter with your cunt up in the air."

Shocked, she looked up into eyes that were an icy blue and so cold that she shivered involuntarily. "No, nothing like that, never!"

The full realization of all that he said came later. Now, whenever she sat across from him at the table, she became so nauseated at the sight of him that she couldn't eat. When she looked in his eyes, she couldn't help remembering a war movie, where this German General with cold pale blue eyes gently stroked a cat while he coolly ordered the execution of women and children.

Laurie knew that something had to be done. Whenever she was alone, she would weep copious tears, so that her eyelids at first became swollen, then dried and caked with salt. Small abrasions appeared on them; the children noticed her changed appearance. The two oldest asked if she had been crying and why she looked so sad. While trying to reassure them, she realized that the situation was not good for them, any more than it was good for her.

Divorce then, was the answer, she realized, but how was it possible when she didn't have a penny to call her own? The bank account and the house were in Kurt's name. Their marriage contract assured her of furniture only. She was a graduate nurse but she hadn't worked since Michael was a baby. How could she work and care for the children? She had no money for a lawyer; legal aid did not exist. A divorce could be granted only if one of them sued for adultery, but they had not been unfaithful to each other. Kurt's preoccupation was his work; he had no energy left for her, nor, as far as she knew, for any other woman. As the complete hopelessness of her situation overcame her, she started to cry quietly.

The supper she managed to put before Kurt was not up to standard so he flew into a rage. "I've had enough of this!" he said. "You have to straighten out." Little did he know how acute was Laurie's suffering, that her tears were mingled into the very soup he ate with such gusto.

All night she cried, till in the morning she called her doctor, told him that her eyelids were bleeding, that she couldn't stop crying. He told her to get in a taxi and meet him at the hospital.

Laurie could not find the help she needed. The chief objective of all concerned was to get her back to her husband and children. A marriage counsellor was engaged who came to the house.

"I feel trapped," Laurie said.

"It's a terrible feeling to be trapped, isn't it?" she replied. Laurie poured out her story, but unfortunately she did not tell of the mental cruelty and verbal abuse. As yet she did not recognize it for what it was, having no idea of how a man talked to a woman. Her own parents had quarrelled so much that it would have been a relief had they separated.

They had a meeting: a therapist, a marriage counsellor, Kurt and Laurie. Towards the end of the meeting Kurt stood up and shouted at Laurie in front of the others. "I've had enough. You're a lousy wife, a lousy cook, a lousy housekeeper and a lousy mother." These were the words that determined the fate of their marriage, for at that moment, Laurie knew that they were through, irrevocably and finally through. As soon as Kurt had said them, she hated him with a passion. She told him she would fabricate an adultery if he wished, she would do anything so long as he would give her a divorce.

Soon the two older children would be in school. A friend had offered to care for the younger ones if she returned to work, and a doctor had offered her a job as a receptionist nearby.

Kurt finally realized that Laurie meant business; a lawyer started proceedings. Laurie sat on a bed in a motel room with a hired actor, she wearing only her undies, he in a semi-state of undress, till a detective stormed in and flashed a picture of the fabricated adultery. Though Laurie had insisted on not removing her slip as she was requested to do, and though all concerned treated her with the respect she so obviously rated, when it was all over, her legs were trembling and she felt as humiliated as if it had all been a real scenario.

Laurie was angry when she realized that Canadians everywhere were forced into such duplicity in order to free themselves from intolerable bondage. It was a travesty of justice, she thought. The alternative was a separation, leaving her essentially still married, doomed either to a life of celibacy, or a lover, never to embrace an honest life.

For a Catholic it meant an even more demeaning and hypocritical situation. A priest is willing to forgive a confessed sin of adultery, but since divorced couples were considered still married in the eyes of the church, remarriage left them excluded from the Sacraments and living in a state of sin. The message was clear, as Laurie was soon to find out. Remain celibate as was expected, be forgiven if you did not, but don't make an honest woman of yourself by remarrying, or you will be ostracized, and if it is done openly and defiantly, you will be ex-communicated.

Though the church was to take a more liberal stand many years later, it could never make amends to those deeply religious Catholics who suffered too much for their faith, for delayed justice is no justice at all.

During the few months of their separation, when Laurie was waiting for the signing of the necessary documents, Kurt made it all too clear that he considered Laurie to be his wife, dropping in whenever he felt like it with a fresh supply of verbal abuse, helping himself to meals, and leaving her with a raging headache. His behaviour served to assure her that she had done the right thing by insisting on a divorce; it would sever the ties and give her the peace she so longed for.

In the meantime, Kurt unleashed his revenge. He sold the house from under Laurie, which was totally unnecessary, then moved her and the children into an apartment in St Bruno. She could have managed the mortgage payments on the house easily. They had only been living there for two years. It was important for the children's welfare that they remain in the same home, go to the same school and retain the same friends. Her heart ached for them, but even if she were to feel guilt for the rest of her life, there was no going back. It was her marriage or her sanity.

Seeing a therapist had been a mistake, because Kurt was telling everyone that Laurie was mentally ill, that she wanted a divorce because she was in love with another man. One would think that her misery would be complete. Kurt said as much.

"My fondest wish is that you will end up in a wheelchair begging me for a handout." But he underestimated Laurie.

She found a good therapist who helped her understand why the divorce happened, to see the inevitability of it, and to understand how parental abuse had preconditioned her to accept abuse from her husband. She realized that it had existed even before their marriage. He also helped her to recognize her strengths and all she had going for her. But most important of all, he made her realize how her falling in love with Tom was not the cause of her estrangement from Kurt, the reverse being closer to the truth.

Laurie had not expected the great feeling of relief that took place in just a few weeks. She was herself again, cheerful, optimistic, and she had a job. Even though it was a night job and part-time, there was enough money to make ends meet. Kurt gave her minimal child support which was enough for food, but she refused a cent for herself. The agreement that she was forced to sign was an insult, giving Kurt too much control. He retained legal custody of the children, giving her physical custody.

Although the children did not have an ideal life, they adjusted better than could have been expected. Kurt and Laurie had not quarrelled or put each other down in their presence, leaving them free to love both parents. Oddly enough, they saw much more of their father now than previously.

In the past Kurt would play poker all night and into the next day, very often having but a few hours to be with his family on the weekend. He also had been making frequent trips out of town, sometimes for a week at a time. Now he saw his children for a full day every weekend and as often as he wished in between, as he had a new job with no travel involved.

Kurt just couldn't understand why all this had happened to him. He considered himself to be a good father and a good husband. After all, he thought, I did not drink or run around, and I always brought home the bacon. The few encounters he had with a woman were very discreet, and only when he was out of town. How could Laurie do this to the children? He had done everything he could to keep the family together, even to the point of offering her an affair. What more could he do? He had begged her to stay for the sake of the children, even promised he would be more considerate, but she was so determined to be what she called free. What made her think she could manage on her own? She would probably beg to come back within a year.

Though Kurt begged Laurie to stay because of the children many times, it never occurred to him that he had not once told her that he couldn't bear to live without her.

Very few Catholics in Quebec had a divorce, Laurie knew of no one herself. She felt somehow that Murdo would be understanding, but she rarely saw him. He was in the Air Force, stationed in Greenwood, Nova Scotia. As for Jimmy, he just preached to her, being more of a priest, she thought, than Murdo ever had been.

Since Laurie would not criticize Kurt, Serafina believed her daughter must be to blame for everything. She would not accept that she was divorced. "You're a Catholic and Catholics can't get a divorce," she said.

Even when Laurie tried to show her the document, signed by the Queen, she waved them away as if they were some sort of forgery or ruse on her part. She heard only what she wanted to hear and dismissed the rest. It was a process of self-righteous denial that she used all her life, to everyone else's complete frustration. Ashamed to acknowledge what she considered Laurie's temporary separation, she tried to hide it from everyone she knew. Laurie felt as if she was disowned, and in a sense, she was.

Serafina claimed to be very liberal-minded in the presence of Protestants and people of different races, saying things like, "We all worship the same God after all," and "we're all God's children," but she ridiculed their customs behind their backs. When a local church burned to the ground, she said with unconcern, "Oh well, it wasn't Catholic."

Oddly enough, it was Catherine, now called Sister James, who was most supportive. Laurie was never to forget her kindness. Though it consisted of only an occasional phone conversation, it lifted her spirits, that is, till Kurt twisted the knife.

He took Michael and Danny to live with him in Germany. The legal agreement specified that he could have physical custody of the two oldest children if he so wished. This did not seem unreasonable at the time since they both had liberal visiting rights, but it never occurred to Laurie that he would leave the country. She had also assumed that if he took them, it would be because he remarried. Having no lawyer to advise her, she trusted Kurt and lost not only her children, but her right to see them.

Though Tom was never far from Laurie's thoughts, she was hesitant about writing to him. Would he want to get involved with her and her children, she wondered? She couldn't visualize that kind of love, nor could she see herself in some sort of affair without commitment, leading nowhere.

For the first time since Laurie could remember, she was not underweight. One morning as she looked in the mirror, she saw a young face, as it had remained relatively unchanged. She remembered how once, Tom had said she was beautiful. Would he still think her so? The radio was on, and as she listened to the haunting melody of "Harbour

Lights," she felt herself once again in Tom's arms. So vivid was the recollection that for a moment she could smell him, part man and part sea.

The tears came unbidden as she took up her pen and wrote to him. She had not heard from him since that valentine three years ago. Sometimes she even doubted that it really did come from him. He was a handsome, virile man, she thought, women would naturally want him. He would desire them and have them. They had probably helped him forget her. But she could desire only him. She wrote him as she would a dear friend and told him basically what had happened since they met, embellishing nothing, nor mentioning how much she had suffered, for she didn't want his pity. That he was her friend was a surety, but that he still loved her was hard to believe.

The months went by without a reply. She joined a social organization, where she met people in the same situation as herself. Though she made friends and dated a little, nothing ever came of it. Some men were of the idea that they could do her a favour by providing sex. One went so far as to say, "After all, you've been accustomed to a beer every day and now the factory is closed." Another asked her if she was not worried because of the absence of her normal biological urges. He was obviously more sophisticated than the beer man, but of the same bent.

She resented those men whose objective was to use a woman temporarily, merely to fill a gap in their lives, until she met several women who wanted nothing more from a man but the very same. They told her they had very strong sexual drives and sought satisfaction even if it meant sleeping with men they did not like or who they would not consider as a mate. Laurie could not judge them as she had not been in their shoes.

They were all in the same boat, however, when it came to concerns about their children. Laurie missed her children so much that they filled her dreams.

She wanted to be with Richard and Linda on weekends and summer vacation. The only way she could do this was to get a job in school health, so she attended university two evenings a week, determined that her children have all the advantages that she could possibly give them. Though she knew there was more to life than hard work, she was prepared to postpone it, and putting herself in God's hands she took one day at a time.

13

Grandma Lila was in her glory! Harding, her son, had just been appointed Deputy Minister of Education for the Province of Nova Scotia. There would be a reception for him in Ottawa, and all the Moffatts were invited. Laurie looked forward to seeing her relations, particularly her cousins, whom she hadn't seen in years.

Once they boarded the Voyageur bus, Richard and Linda became absorbed in a game while she read the latest letter from Michael and Danny. I must have read it at least a dozen times since yesterday, she thought. I wonder if they know how much I love them? I'll write to them as often as I can so they will be sure to know, but right now I must try to be cheerful for Richard and Linda. I must not cry.

"Would you like me to tell you about your cousins?" she said. "Were going to a gathering of the clan."

"What's a clan, Mommy?"

The family reunion was a good idea, giving Laurie the support she so desperately needed. Most of the Moffatts were gifted with a sense of humour so that she found herself laughing in spite of herself. When she saw Richard and Linda darting about with their cousins, having such a good time, she thought about how Michael and Danny would have liked the party. A familiar pain enveloped her.

As she fought to suppress her tears, a man came up to her.

"I believe I am seated beside you at dinner. Allow me to introduce myself. I'm Douglas Whering, a friend of your Uncle Harding's." Laurie pulled herself out of her reverie and tried to be sociable. She wondered what this man with a Mayfair accent was doing at a family reunion, till her uncle caught her eye and winked. Why, they've invited him on my behalf, she thought...how kind.

Douglas had a manner that put Laurie completely at ease. They exchanged pleasantries as he escorted her to the dining room and then assisted her into her chair. He's every inch the gentleman, she thought. Clean cut, Douglas had what Laurie considered to be a Roman nose; not too big for a man, it would have been ugly on a woman. He wore brown which complemented his auburn hair and moustache.

Douglas wanted to know everything about Laurie, not knowing why, except that she appealed to him. Laurie found herself telling him about her children in Germany.

"Did your signed agreement specify that you had liberal visiting rights?" he asked.

"Yes, but Germany is out of the question and he won't send them to me for summer vacation. I made a mistake, now I can't afford a lawyer."

"I'm sure there must be something you can do. I'll look into the matter, if I may." Laurie thanked him. Douglas was a diplomat for the United Nations, and very sensitive about human rights. As the dinner progressed and she learned more about him, she realized that he was perfect for the job.

What struck Laurie as being very different and unusual about Douglas were his eyes. They appeared so innocent for a man who had seen more than forty years, more like the eyes you would expect to see on a very young man who had yet to experience life. They put Laurie in mind of the few times she had come upon a wild deer or a small animal in the forest, that enchanted moment, when looking into the eyes of an innocent, so completely trusting, she wondered how a hunter could do what he set out to do. To change the look in such eyes would be a sacrilege. And yet Douglas could not have been inexperienced as he seemed very relaxed and in command. He behaved with that reserve so typical of the well-mannered Englishman, so that Laurie was unaware at first of his attraction to her.

It was with complete surprise that she received his phone call the next morning, and because she recalled his kind eyes, she agreed to be his guest at an Embassy party that same evening.

"I'll have to wear the same dress as I did yesterday," Laurie said. But her cousin Jennie insisted Laurie borrow anything she wished. Laurie selected a two-piece outfit, consisting of an emerald green v-necked top and long cream-coloured skirt. The emerald green enhanced the green of Laurie's eyes.

"Perfect!" Hazel said. Laurie's Majorca pearl earrings and necklace complemented the outfit. She did her hair in a French twist as opposed to the long loose style she had worn the day before.

"Forget your troubles tonight," Hazel said. "Douglas is an exceptional man. Did you know that he has a black belt in Karate?"

Surprised, Laurie said, "Douglas? He looks so mild-mannered. You could have fooled me!"

Douglas arrived that evening with a Gardenia, a flower that Laurie had never seen before.

"You look enchanting," he said, as he pinned it near her shoulder.

Richard, who had come running into the hall when he heard the bell ring, stood now with the back flap of his pyjamas down, bare bottom exposed, and said, "You should have seen her before, with her hair in curlers. She looked puky." Douglas looked down at him and laughed.

"Sending messages to outer space, was she?"

"You talk funny."

"That's a British accent," Laurie explained.

"Mommy," Linda sighed, "you look like a princess."

Douglas, highly amused with his audience, helped Laurie with her coat and escorted her out to his car. The children waved from a window as Laurie blew them kisses.

So much for my attempts to appear soigné and sophisticated, Laurie thought, a smile on her face.

The party was a lavish affair. Laurie was glad she had taken such pains with her appearance. Bouquets of flowers were tastefully arranged on pedestals, their scent delicate and evasive. An orchestra played all the most popular dance tunes. At one end of the hall was a display of food guaranteed to please even the most discerning palate, a small cascading fountain of punch at its centre.

Though a number of people sought his attention, Douglas stopped only briefly to introduce Laurie and then swept her onto the dance floor. She was pleasantly surprised for he had obviously taken lessons. They glided across the floor to a Viennese waltz and, for a while, Laurie lost herself in the music and the setting. She was having a good time, that is, until the orchestra played "Harbour Lights." A nearly physical pain swept over her, like a burning hopelessness. She felt like running, preferably from life itself, yet she could do nothing.

So expressive was her face, that Douglas noticed at once and solicitously led her to a chair.

"You have that look again," he said, "the same look in

your eyes that I saw when I first met you." Laurie hadn't realized that she had been wearing her love for Tom as a banner on her sleeve, so she apologized.

"No apology required," Douglas said. "I only wish you could let me help to release the haunted look from your eyes. Will you let me try, Laurie?"

As the evening progressed, Laurie realized that Douglas wanted to see a lot of her, so it was only fair to tell him about her feelings for Tom. Douglas not only gratefully accepted her gift of friendship, but he convinced her that it made him very happy.

"Please use me," he said, making her laugh, till they soon were talking up a storm. Laurie had been starved for conversation and Douglas had not had such rapport with anyone in a long time.

They were seated on a comfortable lounge, Douglas telling Laurie about his parents' home in Scotland, when Laurie noticed that a beautiful woman was giving Douglas the eye. She waited till it became obvious to them both, and then said, "She's giving you the 'come on,' Douglas."

"Yes, I suppose she is," he answered, with such savoir faire, as if to imply that it happened every day, and what a bore it all was. Laurie, not bored in the least, realized that it was one in the morning; the weekend was coming to a close.

When Douglas said good night to Laurie, he did not kiss her, but taking her hand in his, asked if she would accompany him to church service in the morning, and afterwards if she and the children would have lunch with him. Laurie, never having been invited to church before, found the idea refreshing. And yet she hesitated. Douglas intervened.

"I belong to the Church of Scotland, but we may go to Catholic Mass if you wish."

"No, this is something I can do for you, Douglas. We will go to your church. But are you sure you want the kids at lunch? They can be a handful; you aren't accustomed to children."

"Your children are enchanting, Laurie. Don't give it another thought. I'll pick you up for the eleven o'clock service and afterwards we'll return for the children."

As Laurie knelt in church the next morning, Douglas beside her, she prayed for Michael and Danny, asking God to bring them back to her. She hoped that Kurt would become disillusioned with Germany and return to Montreal. She also prayed for Tom.

"If it is not in your plan to bring him back to me," she prayed, "then be merciful and release me from this longing."

It had rained earlier, a fine Spring drizzle, but by the time Laurie and Douglas, children in tow, had lunch, the sun broke through giving every promise of a fine day. Crocuses were in evidence everywhere and the trees were heavy with bud.

Douglas took them on a tour of the Nation's Capital, stopping for tea on the way back. He then waited for them to collect their bags and drove them to the bus station. While the children scrambled aboard, Douglas said goodbye to Laurie, promising to write and to visit Montreal whenever he could.

"Friends?" he said.

"Always," Laurie replied. But when the bus pulled out, her thoughts were far away on the open sea, to wherever Tom might be, and her heart would not let go.

Douglas wrote to Laurie every week without fail. His impeccable English was a pleasure to read, his work most interesting, but otherwise his life seemed uneventful. He said he would be in Montreal for a few days at Easter to see her and to see a friend of his, a lawyer. I have the utmost confidence that something can be done about your children, the letter read.

The following week, he checked in at the Mt Royal hotel and drove to Laurie's apartment. He brought fresh Spring blooms and an Easter basket filled with goodies for the children. He also brought Laurie a bottle of "Muguet Des Bois" eau de parfum, having recalled Laurie say that her favourite flower was Lily of the Valley.

Apparently, they make it only once a year in the Spring," he said.

That evening, he took Laurie to one of the finest restaurants in Montreal. She began to feel guilty.

"You're doing so much for me, and I so little by comparison," she said.

"On the contrary, you're giving me much more than you realize, Laurie."

This was the night he kissed her, a gentle sweet kiss. He contained his passion, and Laurie felt warm because of it. She knew he was probably the best man she had ever known.

Easter dinner at Laurie's place was as traditional as she was: a ham decorated with pineapple and cherries, glazed with maple syrup, and lemon meringue pie. The flowers Douglas had brought graced the table and yellow candles cast a soft glow. Laurie wore a mauve dress which accentuated her dark hair and Douglas, getting into the spirit of the occasion, had worn whatever whatever he could find in his wardrobe that looked a bit Easter, a pale lemon cardigan with a lemon and brown tie. The children wore their best, already smudged with chocolate.

The next day, after seeing his friend, Douglas came back with good news.

"Just a few minutes in court," he said, "and a letter will be on its way to Germany informing your ex-husband that, should he not send the children to you for their summer vacation, he will be fined and jailed on his return to Canada."

Laurie was overjoyed. "I might have them this summer!"

"Unless he chooses to ignore the order, but if as you say, he plans to return to Canada, he will most likely comply. I have something else of importance to tell you, Laurie. I have been transferred to England for at least two years, but rest assured, I shall contact you regularly."

When Laurie said goodbye to Douglas, she knew with a certainty he would keep in touch. Since there had not been much she could count on in her past, save hardship and suffering, it was a good feeling.

When she was not thinking about Michael and Danny, Laurie wondered where Tom was, fabricating a myriad of excuses as to why he had not answered her letter. That he just didn't want to become involved at all occurred to her often, but her heart could not fully accept this now. In the stillness of the night, when the stars stood diamond sharp, she would stand on her balcony and recall his image: his laughing blue eyes, so openly loving when he looked at her, and his crooked grin that tore at her heart. Overcome with longing she remembered the gypsy's words of so long ago.

"Your heart will always be hungry," she had said. Was she to feel this ache for the rest of her days? How could she bear it?

Meanwhile, back in Germany, Kurt realized that caring for two children was restricting him in ways that he had not foreseen, most notably by putting a damper on his love life. When he received the court order demanding he send Michael and Danny to their mother for summer vacation, he was alarmed, yet relieved. The matter had been taken out of his hands and he could thereby save face.

Not only did he dispatch the children promptly, for the duration of their schooling, but he developed a new respect for Laurie. The respect was compounded when a letter from his children informed him that Laurie had completed several university courses.

The old house by the river was on the same street where she lived as a girl. It was an attached cottage, very old and in need of repair, but the down payment was only a thousand dollars. Laurie disliked the house but it was the only one within her means. Dark, with layers of old wallpaper, a depressing shade of yellow-green paint everywhere, she at first rejected it. But it was the fireplace that changed her mind.

A fireplace is a blessing, she thought. It provides not only warmth on damp between-season days, but a feeling of well-being, an aura of romance and history; a blazing fire could cheer or it could provide the perfect setting for deep and rewarding thought.

She set to work. Soon the place was bright and inviting. She felt proud of her home as she had done all the painting and wallpapering herself.

There were other reasons why she felt good about herself. Due to her university courses, she not only earned a higher salary, but a position in school health. This allowed her to be with her children on weekends and summer vacation, providing time as well for her to continue with her courses. She believed, nonetheless, that she could not do it without God's help.

She gave thanks and prayed for strength on awakening. Having been on her own for two years, it felt more like ten, but she believed that the mysterious force that kept her looking young and gave her energy was somehow related to her humble acceptance of God.

She returned to the island as soon as she could, and looked for Janus, not expecting to see him again. When he came soaring in and perched on his rock, she was heartened. He looked much heavier and older, like the Grandfather of all seagulls, but it was he. Not only did she recognize his familiar markings, but he showed no fear of her, having imprinted her image on his memory.

"You're here, Janus, I never expected to see you again."

He turned his head sharply and gave her a penetrating look as if to say, "and why not?"

Laurie laughed. "You always have the last word, Janus," then she took up her pen to write.

Writing came much easier since she last saw Tom. It must be because she had suffered much and loved more, thereby gaining empathy, that double-edged sword enabling us to feel another's pain.

As she looked to shore, and recalled the gypsy who told her fortune, she wished to see her again, this wise woman, who had recognized the hunger in her eyes. But the gypsies no longer camped there. Some houses were going up; soon the fields would be gone, the ponds where they found tadpoles in the summer and skated in the winter. But worst of all, dredging was to start to make the St Lawrence Seaway. How would it affect the island? she wondered.

As the wind moved through the grass, dragonflies darted with fluttering transparent wings, and a million silvery highlights danced on blue, and pink, and green. Enchanted, she lay back and thought of the Indian girl who married George Moffatt. Borne backward in time, she tried to visualize how life might have been for her, long ago.

14

The St Lawrence river between St Lambert
and Montreal, 1809
(The Story of the Island of Stone)

They paddled leisurely toward Ile à la Pierre, the white man and the Indian girl with the papoose on her back. Their eyes met often and they smiled. She was lovely to look at and glowed with her new-found motherhood.

She thought about her people who, long ago, had always come here to fish and to gather the special stone to make arrowheads and tools. Then the French came to gather stones to build their houses. The Mohawks and the Oneidas were hidden in the bush; they killed a priest and thirteen men, some of them soldiers. The white man had called it 'a massacre,' she thought, but when they burnt our village to the ground, killing many, was it not a massacre?

And they call us savages, though they taught our braves to use fire water and how to take a woman by force, something that our braves had never done, for to do so would bring great dishonour to our people. They say we were Godless pagans, but they invaded our land and did not call it stealing, killed more animals than they needed to eat and called it pleasure.

We see the great Manitou everywhere and in everything. They must go to church to see Him. When the missionaries made our people Christian, they taught us the Ten Commandments. One of them is "you shall not steal." When I asked the blacksuit why they stole our land, he said it was not stealing because it did not belong to us. I told him that if our warriors went to England and took their land it would be stealing. He said that was not the same thing. When I asked how it was different, I could tell by his eyes that he did not believe his answers and he felt ashamed. I liked him because he felt this shame.

Her father was against the marriage even though George had considerable wealth, but when he said he would one day buy the Island of Stone, he permitted the marriage. "He will buy it from those who stole it from us," he said. Her mother said little, but she understood why her daughter's heart flew towards the man with eyes like a summer sky and hair like corn silk.

They disembarked and "Talks a Lot," for that was her name, set up camp. Her mother had named her "Talks a Lot" because as a baby she never cried, and rarely spoke, even as a child. Not that she could not talk if she so wished. It was just that there was more to hear and more to see if she did not talk. When they poured water on her head to make her Christian, the water Spirit gave her the name Mary.

She was the one who cared for the man called George when he had the pox. It was on his first trip into the Athabaska, when he was so ill that the others feared to go near him. She had remained near him and lay large pieces of soft moss soaked in herb water on his tortured skin. It soothed the itching and took the heat from his body. She drank only water, because she feared that if she left him to go for food, he would scratch and become scarred. She gave him a drink made with the juice of a bark.

At the end of the second day she had a vision. In this vision, the sun and the moon were both in the sky, because when the sun rose the moon did not go. Instead, they joined together. At the moment of their joining, a wolf cried his lonely song. The wolf was the sign of her mother's clan. She knew from the vision that she belonged to the white man. If he wanted her, he would get well again and reach out to her, like the sun to the moon.

In the brief period of awareness, during the first few days, George opened his eyes to see her lovely face and her sweet smile. He felt her gentle touch, and took the vision with him into the land of dreams. When the fever left him, and he awoke to find she was more than a dream, how could he not want her?

Now Mary watched George as he turned over rocks in the water to choose some of the small creatures for bait. Then he waded out above the rapids and threw his line. The large rock bass were plentiful, as well as the eel, and they tasted delicious.

As he waited he looked back at his wife and was filled with pride. She was a good wife, had given him a fine son whom he had named Lewis. He had built her a house but she had trouble adapting to other ways. She was always eager for a trip to the island or to accompany him on a forest hunt, but his business interests had allowed less time for such in the past year.

It wasn't that she could not learn, as she was bright, but she considered the white man's ways foolish. Dressed in white women's clothes, she appeared awkward, but dressed in her doeskin as she was now, she looked graceful and appealing. He didn't mind her quiet nature because even when she wasn't talking and her face still, her moods stirred like a current under calm water. It was beautiful to see.

The women who knew her were nice enough, but in a patronizing way, and she felt it. This angered George, but what else could he expect, knowing how they thought. He called them washed-out Bible punchers. Often, they tried to change her, till he made them back off. They couldn't hold a candle to her in the wild, and as far as religion went she had more of God in her little finger than all of those so-called Christians put together! When she accompanied him on expedition to the Athabaska, she was indispensable and he was fiercely proud of her.

Mary had a fire ready and had fed the baby. He brought in a fish and gave it to her. After he had eaten, he lay back on a boulder, telling her of his dreams. He wanted a train to go through St Lambert, across the river to this island. From the island there would be a ferry to Montreal. The settlers found it a hardship to cross the ice in winter and it was difficult by boat in summer because of the rapids. He wanted the people in the fort and surrounding areas to buy his goods. Part owner of a major Montreal supply house for the fur trade, he had succeeded in establishing an agency of the Hudson's Bay Company. Soon he would be receiving more seaborne goods than any other firm in the Canadas. He told her that he would teach his son Lewis everything.

Mary thought about what was said. She, too, must teach her son the ways of her people, for she wanted him to be proud that he was Oneida. Lewis would be an important man who would never know hunger. Would he be the son she hoped him to be, or would he think like a white man only? These thoughts weighed heavily on her heart, but she was determined that nothing should spoil the day, for after all, was she not happy as she watched George play with their son, and when she saw the light in his eyes that burned only for her.

The baby, having been satiated with milk, dozed off. When George turned towards Mary, he saw milk dripping from her nipple. Curiously he caught it on his finger and tasted it.

"Mmm," he said, "creamy good." They both laughed, and she invited him to her breast for more. Soon her small cries of pleasure mingled with the bird sounds as he gently removed her clothing and she, his. They retired to a place where the moss was soft and resilient, in a recess between two boulders.

The setting and the feel of the moss against George's skin fired him, till his love lust became a primordial force, stronger than anything he had experienced before. He shouted to the sky as he rode her. Like a wild man he reverted to animal sounds and roared into the wind startling a community of birds, who fluttered upward in unison creating such a din, that he collapsed in laughter, Mary laughing with him.

15

It was unusually warm for a September day. Laurie wanted to visit the island just once more before the cold days settled in. The shoreline in every direction was a sunny haze of red and gold. Soon the first windy day would come and the leaves would start to shudder. Fall was her favourite season and it would start at any time now. Some people see Autumn and Fall as the same, but she didn't see it that way. The leaves attain their full beauty in Autumn, but once the winds come they start to quiver as if touched by music. With abandon they break loose and spiral downward in shades of amber, garnet, coral and jade. There comes a scent in the air like no other, a rustling sound and a crunching under her feet. She loved to walk, breathing deep of that mysterious elixir that brought colour to her cheeks and a spring to her walk. Ah yes! Fall has a particular, moving sound.

But it was also a reminder that time flowed by and she was being left behind, never knowing what it really was that she hungered for. Some philosophers say that because we hunger for God, it is proof that He exists. But she needed no proof of that. Several times in the lowest point in her life, God was revealed to her. One feels God or he doesn't, she thought. It was as simple as that, for no one by reason could find God. And yet she looked over the water and hungered.

She heard the sound of oars dipping. Someone was coming towards the island. She stood up, shading her eyes, looking for the intruder, and then she saw his golden hair. She waited for him and when he smiled, her heart gave a single, great leap!

They loved on Moffatt's Island and Laurie discovered what people have fought and died for since the time before time. They nested in a hidden mossy spot and their loving was a sacrament.

"I've been looking for you," Tom said. "I looked towards the island every time I came into port and I have never stopped loving you."

His mother had died and he had found Laurie's letter among her things. Her memory had been very bad in her last years and she had simply forgotten it. He said he didn't care if Laurie had a dozen children and they laughed about that.

"Well, perhaps a dozen would have scared me a bit," he said.

On his first visit he arrived with his duffle bag laden with exotic gifts from many ports, enthralling the children with stories of seafaring men and their hilarious adventures. They adored him.

As for herself, Laurie wondered at her new-found sensuality. Since Tom had said the magic words, "why don't you try getting on top," her pleasure had increased and, as the weeks slipped by, became so intense that she cried out involuntarily. She was now a woman of the fourth wave.

"Surely it's not possible to have more than four," she said.

"Oh yes it is." he replied.

"But it would probably kill me! I might have heart failure. I'm afraid to even try." Then they would collapse, laughing.

It was not solely because of the mechanics of sex that she became fulfilled, but because somewhere in her brain, she was convinced that Tom loved the sight and smell of her body. She felt proud of her sexual equipment and abandoned herself to sensation.

He sought no pleasure that he could not share with her, indeed he would postpone his own, waiting till her needs met his. He couldn't get enough of touching her, caressing her, arousing her and having her. Now she felt herself desiring him at inopportune times, on the highway, at the table, in the market and all manner of places, till she feared she was becoming a nymphomaniac.

"Is this normal? Do other people do it this often?" she asked, as she lay with her head in the curve of his neck.

"It's new for you and in a sense you're making up for lost time. I'm a lucky guy. You're a very sensuous woman."

"Me? Sensuous! Really?" She was filled with the wonder of it. "Have you loved a lot of women?"

"A few, but every time you love it's different and I've never had the time to indulge her love for very long. It will be different for us, Laurie. I'll do anything so that we won't be apart for long even if it means getting other work."

When she asked him about the women in his life she was sorry that she did, for although she wanted to know, she didn't realize that the telling would cause her a strange kind of physical pain, that seeped through her abdomen. He told her about the first girl, a tiny Tahitian. "She waited for me every time I came into port, she would sleep only with me till I left and when I said goodbye I gave her whatever money I had left in my pockets. She never cared if it was a little or a lot." Laurie knew the girl must have loved him.

Then he told her there had been many whores and about the very expensive brothel in Louisiana, where the madam had called upstairs, "Girls, gentlemen callers." She laughed as she pictured the group of rough sailors feeling out of place in all the luxury. Shocked at the idea of whores, she was intrigued all the same. They were no longer only the stuff of novels. This was real and she wanted to understand.

"A sailor is not allowed the luxury of extended involvement," he said, "but we long for a human touch and female companionship, no matter how brief." A little seed of worry imbedded itself in Laurie's brain, but she pushed it aside, too absorbed with her happiness. But it wouldn't go away and Tom was going to sea again.

He had not talked about marriage, and she was reluctant to be the first to bring it up. But the next time he came into port, she managed to talk about it in a roundabout way. To her relief, he said that, of course, they would be married, but he never dwelt on the subject for long.

He was wonderful company, pitching in with the housework, "getting everything shipshape" as he put it. There was only one thing lacking. At times she longed for some conversation on a deeper level, but when she tried to bridge this gap she found their opinions were usually at odds. This was something she could accept but he could not. He felt an absolutism, whereas she enjoyed a quest for truth, like a door forever opening onto another.

She told herself there was no such a thing as a perfect relationship, just as there was no such a thing as a perfect job.

Most of Tom's time in port was when the river was iced and so he was with them at Christmas time. But Laurie didn't want to live with him until the wedding date had been set, so he kept his digs at the seamen's hotel. That they made love at all, outside of marriage, was frowned upon. To do so in the same house where there were young children, unthinkable.

One day in the late Spring, Tom came to tell her that he had accepted a job as stevedore, which meant she would no longer have to be alone for months at a time. It was the right thing to do, he said, as it was time he settled down. They made plans to be married in late June.

During the next month, she was so exuberant with marriage plans that at first she didn't notice a change in Tom, but he soon became noticeably more quiet and preoccupied.

"Is anything wrong?" Laurie asked.

"No, everything's fine. I just have to become accustomed to my new way of life. I'm lucky to get the job I have. The pay is good and the men a good lot to work with."

In spite of his reassurance he became a different man before her eyes, and now, when she remarked on the change, he became defensive, almost irritable. When she suggested they go out to the island for a picnic, and maybe some fishing, he jumped at the idea. Once there, however, he became despondent. She noticed that he often looked towards the ships with his spy glass, remarking on each, as to where they had been or which one was soon to leave and for which port. It suddenly dawned on her.

"You wish you were back at sea, don't you," she said. When he turned to her, the look on his face was enough to tear Laurie's heart out. "O Tom! I want you to be happy. You don't have to give up what you love most for me. It wasn't my idea at all, it was yours."

"It wouldn't be fair to you and the children," he said. "You deserve a full-time husband."

"But lots of seamen are married and I'd rather have you home happy and full of zest for living a few weeks at a time than be here every day wishing you were somewhere else. Eventually, you would resent me. Don't you see?"

By the time they reached home, he was his old self again. They agreed that he would try to get on his old ship. It did not turn out as they had hoped, because although he was able to reinstate himself in the union, being well known and liked, the only ship that needed him was making a long run and it meant he would see even less of her than previously.

"Take it," Laurie said, "until there's another opening. We love each other, and love can wait." But to her distress Tom suggested that they postpone the marriage until his return, as he would be gone for four months.

"I just wouldn't feel right about leaving you for that long so soon. You might have regrets."

"How could I have regrets, knowing that my husband, whom I love dearly, would be coming home to me?"

"Among my mates there were many married men, but only one remained faithful to his wife. I would like to prove to myself that I have what it takes to make you a good and faithful husband."

His mind was set. Laurie tried to comfort herself with the thought that he just wasn't ready yet, but that all would end up well. There was no doubt in her mind that he loved her.

But now she had to consider other possibilities. Suppose he never was ready for a marriage commitment. Would it mean he didn't love her enough? She wondered if she could accept the situation as it was, provided he was faithful to her. But how would she know? I would know because we have been so close, came a reply from within. To find the answers to some of her questions she had to let him go without guilt and without making her any promises.

When she said goodbye to him on the same dock where she had sat on that fatal day over six years ago, his kiss left her no doubt that she was the focal point in his life, but whereas it confirmed her with his love, it devoured her with his passion and she knew with a sinking heart that his need for her would be too great.

16

At first his letters came frequently, so she could tell he had written several while at sea, and posted them right away in port. How she looked forward to those letters! She read them quickly on her return from work, then quietly and slowly before sleep. He had a good pen and he captured in words the flavour of a place and his feelings towards her. Some of his letters were a bit raunchy, perhaps, but this was a part of the Tom she loved.

When the letters arrived less often, she accepted his reasons for she was not a demanding person, but when they changed she noticed immediately—not that the wording was any different, but they were shorter in content as if he dashed them off in a hurry. Hurt and bewildered, she loved to think that writing to her was the highlight of his day, as it was when she wrote to him. However, just when she became worried to the point of distraction, she received another long and wonderful letter full of reassurance in which he said he loved her, that he would always love her, and that she must never stop believing it. This was in February. It was the last letter she received from him.

One can well imagine what kind of hell Laurie went

through during that time. It seemed as if God had abandoned her. A severe cold snap was in progress. The trees creaked, the freezing sap in the hardwoods popped and the mythical Grundoons squealed under every footfall. It snowed often and heavily and as Laurie looked from her window, it felt as if the cold was seeping into her veins. She felt numb and shivered.

Tom and she had agreed that at a specific time once a week, they would send out thoughts to each other and record their feelings if they felt they had received a message. Although they had an open mind where telepathy was concerned, they knew it was an experiment. He gave her a world time clock as a present, "just so you won't be sending me deep messages at four in the morning while I'm snoring up a storm." he said. They had laughed about it a lot.

The last time he was away, it was she who once received a strong impression identical to the one he sent. Surprised, yet still sceptical, he put it down to coincidence. But her belief was reinforced.

During this time, Laurie clung pitifully to the hope of a telepathic message. There was always the possibility that Tom was sick or injured, or that something disastrous had prevented a letter from reaching her. She became very ill herself in March with pneumonia, and at the height of her fever, set her time clock. After sending a message of love and longing through a mist of tears, she waited to no avail. That night she awoke after a very strange dream, a dream so vivid that it needed no recording. She felt peaceful and happy.

They were seated on wooden chairs facing each other and they were bent forward in conversation. She could see the man with the strange kind face as through a mist. He was telling her how he had grown to respect her and how she had brought special meaning into his life. He seemed to be leading up to something. Oh no, she thought, he's going to ask me to marry him, but I can't because I don't love him!

Before she could stop him, he asked her to marry him. She said that she was sorry, but she couldn't, that she liked him a lot and hoped they could always be friends. The man wept as he slowly opened a small piece of white paper and held it in the palm of his hand. On it lay a beautiful diamond. His tears fell upon it, scattering bits of light before her eyes. He continued to talk as he wept.

Now if you can imagine for a moment that all the words of love that you could ever want to hear and all the longing ever spent, were laid before you as a gift straight from the heart, then this is what he gave to her. She felt the sincerity of his poignant message and she became deeply moved. What he said to her exactly, she could never recall, because what he said was too lofty for language to reach. And yet he said it.

As he continued to talk a wonderful peace crept into her being and filled her with love. Then she said to him, "I would be proud and happy to be your wife. At first I did not understand, but your words have opened a door for me."

Laurie tried to fathom the meaning of her dream but she couldn't understand. Who was this man, and how could a dream be so real that it left her feeling the same way on awakening?

Savouring the dream, she went through those days mechanically, knowing from previous experience that time had a healing quality. She was still apprehensive and still suffered, but gradually a resignation took hold of her.

In the Spring, she watched Tom's ship as it came into port and to her surprise her feelings engulfed her. Although she told herself she should not go to meet it, she went anyway, hoping for she knew not what. She watched till the crew disembarked and when she saw that Tom was not among them, she approached one of the last men to leave and queried him. He told her gently that Tom had remained in Tahiti, but he was reluctant to say more. Laurie could see the pity in his eyes and she felt humiliated.

Tom had told her about the girl, so she guessed he was with her. Now that her worst fears were confirmed, a subtle change took place in Laurie. Her pain and humiliation turned to anger. At first she decided she had been played for a fool, but after reading his last letter, she conceded that it was more likely something happened to him that he had not foreseen and that his intentions towards her had been sincere.

After all, what did she know? Her knowledge of men was extremely limited. He had told her that every love was different and it was true that she had loved in different ways: as a child, as an adolescent, a wife and mother, and as a mature woman. It was important, though, to love with honesty. She told herself that never again would she give her heart so freely. She had her children, her career, her home and most of all she still had that sense of wonder from season to season, for no matter how much she endured, she never became hard.

Laurie no longer thought in terms of what she wanted, but thought instead of how she could make the best of herself. She started on a new phase of her life, a wiser, self-sufficient woman, neither happy nor sad, but content for the first time in years. It felt good.

When Laurie went to the island that summer she noticed a change in Janus. He looked bedraggled, as if he no longer had the energy to preen himself, and though he came close to her, he was no longer interested in the titbits she threw him.

She was wondering why there were not many gulls around, when she was startled by a deafening noise. It frightened her and caused a commotion among the birds who nervously took flight. The two smaller islands, Fisherman's and Boys, further down river and nearer the bridge, were almost bare of birds. She could see Mr Payette minnowing off Fisherman's Island. He was a permanent fixture thereabouts; sometimes when the wind was right, she could hear him singing the old Voyageur songs. He can't feel much like singing now, she thought with a pang of regret.

They had started to dredge for the seaway down below Victoria Bridge. It was dynamite that caused the roar and soon the work crew would approach this area. She wondered if she would be able to come here again. Surely, they could make access to the island possible, she thought, but she suddenly realized that except for a few fishermen, nobody came here. It was not like it used to be years ago, when people came for picnics, lit bonfires and set off fireworks for the Queen's birthday. Few took any interest now, besides the fishermen.

"Why do men destroy that which they love the most, Janus?" she asked. He turned his head sharply and looked at her. They both knew the answer.

They destroy that which they love the most because they compete with God for power, a foolish game they are bound to lose.

"Poor Janus," she said, "I wish I could help you. You look as if you've had a hard time."

He descended from his perch, waddled toward her, closer than he had ever come before, and then raising his wings with a lot of effort, he struggled into the air, circled around her head several times, crooning a long poignant gull song, then he soared higher than she had ever seen him go, and descended quietly and gloriously spinning, to crash into the rapids. "Goodbye, my dear friend," she said. "Thank you for listening."

And then she wept, not for Janus, for he had had a good life, and left with wonderful flair, but for the passing of time that swept that which was good and holy along with the bad, to be scattered like so much foam upon the water.

That day she thought about her own mortality. She wondered about her ancestors, but especially the mystery of the Indian maiden whom George Moffatt had married. Why was her name obscured in history and when did she die? Was she cast aside to die of a broken heart?

The island held her secret.

What Shall We Say to the Children?

When I was a child I heard a happy song
about the best things in life being free,
but the river no longer flows by the shore
where I tied my boat to a tree.

It takes money now and lots of time
to find some air that's clean,
far from the smoke, far from the noise,
where flowers grow by a stream.

Who will find strawberries in the field again
and bring tadpoles home in a jar?,
for gone are the fields and gone is the pond,
and another is much too far.

Where shall we watch the sun go down
and see the wondrous Northern Lights?
Now there are walls to hide the sun,
and the moon, and starfilled nights.

Do you hear the song upon the wave
that weeps for the earth and all things wild?
It is the song that the children sing,
for the cry of a whale is the cry of a child.

17

The Island of Stone

The Indian woman Mary sat on the island and thought about the past and the present. As she thought, she worked on a tasselled deerskin jacket that she was making for her son Lewis. It was the finest she had ever made and it was nearly finished. Lewis would soon be seven years old and he would soon be a man. It was to be his gift. She knew he would wear it when he went hunting with his father and sometimes he would wear it when he wanted to show that he was part Oneida, for she had given him this pride in her people. He was a good son.

But there was another reason why this jacket had to be the finest, with the best beadwork. She felt that her spirit would not be here for very long and that soon she would join her ancestors.

She had tried very hard to be a good wife for George, her husband. She had worn the white women's clothing even though it was not comfortable and had lived in his house. She would rather wear her deerskin and sleep in a tepee, wanted to leap on a horse many times when the mood took her, to feel the wind in her hair and the sun on her face. But she loved her husband, so she waited and did once in a while, what she wanted to do every day.

She was glad to have a house in the winter, because she had seen a lot of suffering in the two coldest months, when the old ones died and food was scarce.

On the rare occasions when George introduced her to a white woman, Mary could think of nothing to say. They thought her to be savage and she knew it. She felt by the way they looked at her, that they expected her to do something wrong and waited for it to happen. Once she pictured herself taking a scalp from her pocket and showing it to them, so that they all screamed and fainted. She smiled at the secret thought.

It was true, though, that the ladies thought her needlework to be beautiful, for it was obvious that it was more than well done. They tolerated her because her husband was an important man.

Mary thought of all these things and then she spoke. "I must return to my people before my spirit is set free. Would they remember me, the girl they called 'Talks a Lot'?"

She coughed and the cough shook her body till she felt very weak. When she had become thin, George had noticed and called a doctor. He had given her a medicine for the cough that went and came back again like a thief, to rob her of her strength and make her tired. She knew she had the lung sickness because she had seen George's eyes as he stroked her hair. She wanted to be here on the island just once more, for this was the place of memories that burned her heart with beautiful fire.

The Anglican priest had taught her about Heaven, but when she had asked where Heaven was he did not know, nor did anyone else. They looked up at the sky and thought it might be there. She did not think it was there. She knew it was in the forest and on the mountain and here on the island where she had been most happy, with the river flowing by, her son in her arms and her husband beside her.

In her hand she clutched her Baptism certificate, her passport to heaven, She felt her soul at peace because she had known love in full measure. Mary was ready to begin the long journey home.

18

Moffatt's Island, 1846

George Moffatt stood on the island and watched the ships go to and from the port of Montreal. He was successful beyond his wildest dreams, but his dreams were for Canada. His company handled a cargo of fifteen foreign ships, one of which he owned. Soon his son Lewis would open his own branch in Toronto.

He had so many interests that it was necessary to escape now and then for a few hours of solitude and what better place than here. He and his long-time friend Gillespie now had an insurance company to run. Past director of the bank of Montreal, he was now director of the St Lawrence and Atlantic Railway, running from St Lambert and soon to reach Portland, Maine. He led in the formation of the exclusive St James Club and he was busy in his support of McGill University.

His legislative career had begun years ago. He introduced a bill in favour of the High School of Montreal and another on behalf of the Grey Nuns. His thoughts switched from politics to fur and wheat, hardware and dry goods, to banking, insurance, mining, railways and land speculation. There was so much more to be done, but when he came to the island the pressures of work escaped him and he felt refreshed.

He bought the island as he had planned and his colleagues wondered why it was so important to him. They made jokes about Moffatt's Island, not realizing that the happiest moments of his life were spent right here. The island refreshed him. It was a haven from business. He could be alone with Mary, for if, as he believed, a spirit goes wherever it wills, then for sure she was always here.

A tear splashed on the stones as George Moffatt remembered the first time he had seen the sweet Indian girl who had captured his heart, with her soft eyes, her shy smile and her gentle touch.

19

Laurie has always loved Christmas and begins its preparation at least two months in advance by baking her fruit cakes and making plans. She chooses gifts all through the year whenever she can get the most value for her money and stores them away in a box under her bed. One month before the big day, having forgotten what was in there, she enjoys spreading out the gifts and matching them to the appropriate person on her list. She can't afford to be self-indulgent, but for just a little while the gifts are hers and she takes pleasure in looking at them. She is fully occupied all December with cleaning, decorating, wrapping and finally the purchase of the tree.

A few days before Christmas, she sets up the tree, the most difficult task. The next day, after all the branches thaw and settle, she arranges the lights in a symmetrical fashion, another task that usually involves more than she anticipates. The third evening she decorates, a more pleasurable experience. Then, taking deep breaths of elixir of evergreen, she sits back to enjoy the wonder of it all.

On Christmas Eve, she puts the Infant in the crèche that until now has been significantly empty, after which, while listening to carols, she melts into a state of happy sentiment.

The children come and go in a frenzy of activity, giggling and conspiring in their rooms amidst paper and tape, never stopping long enough to really savour the mood. They no longer believe in Santa Claus, but Laurie does in a way, because odd-looking packages appear under the tree to tug at her heart strings. Though she has often been lonely at this time, wishing for a mate to share her special moments, she cannot be sad, because she knows that compared to so many she has so much.

There are things that she believes but these are not necessarily things that she knows, for believing is not knowing, it is Faith, universal, wonderful. But spare her from those who think they are *right*!

And so when she listens to carols, she says a prayer of thanksgiving, and the believing makes Christmas that much better.

This holiday would also be special because Douglas would be a part of it, or so she had thought. He had come to Montreal on a short visit and planned to stay till after the holidays, but his plans had to be changed because his father had a severe heart attack which made it imperative that he return to Scotland. Laurie saw Douglas in a different light than she had nearly two years ago. Time was just about the only thing that could heal when it came to matters of the heart, but just when she thought that she might be ready for a new experience, he had to leave.

"I saw it coming, Laurie," he said. "We've only been together for two weeks and had we become closer you may have been hurt. As it is, I'll try to get a transfer back to Ottawa, no matter how long the wait. I want to return, but I can't promise you anything because I don't want to disappoint you."

That evening, feeling let down, she yelled at Douglas who wasn't there to hear her, "but I *am* disappointed and I *am* hurt!" But she was glad they had not become intimate, for she would feel a lot worse. She thought perhaps they might never cross the line of friendship, as she had been down that road once too often.

She had secretly been knitting him a sweater for Christmas and now she sent it with him, boxed and wrapped. She had done something else. On impulse, she wove some hair from her head into the wool near his heart for she did not want him to forget her.

The Christmas card Douglas sent was an ordinary one but the letter was long. He told her that he loved the sweater, he hoped she would have a happy Christmas and that he missed her.

Laurie was having some modest success with her writing which kept her busy and left no free time that winter.

Spring came as a surprise once again, and the very same day that she looked from her kitchen window to see the first crocus in the rock garden, was the day the doorbell rang and Tom stood there.

20

He looked thinner than before and somehow older, though he still retained his rugged good looks. Obviously uncomfortable, he couldn't have been more uncomfortable than Laurie was. She waited for him to speak.

"Please," he said, "I just want to talk to you and then I'll leave." She allowed him to enter, but when he reached out to take her hand she shrank from him.

They sat down at opposite ends of the small room and he then said, "I've been through hell, Laurie."

"*You've* been through hell! It's been *two* years! What could you possibly say that could make any difference?"

"The woman in Tahiti had my son and I didn't know about it. She was sick and scraping a living on the docks to care for him. What could I do? I couldn't just leave them like that! They needed my help."

"And what about me, who am I? You could have told me. I would have understood. Did you live with her...were you intimate?" He didn't answer and the implication felt like a hot pain in her gut.

"Who helped who?" she rasped, becoming irrational.

"I tried not to and for a time succeeded, but she loves

me and I'm afraid I was not as strong as I wanted to be. But it wasn't serious, it was just sex Laurie... nothing like what we have. I'd give anything for it not to have happened."

"You should have written, not kept me waiting and suffering for so long. Believe it or not, I can get sick too."

Tom looked pained. He lowered his head onto his hands. "Do you think it was easy for me? I just wanted to care for my son until his mother got well, but as time went on, she came close to death. She's better now but still weak. I finally got her family to take over. At first they would have nothing to do with her because of her reputation as a prostitute, but eventually the boy won them over."

"Well, I've got news for you, Tom. I felt close to death too! I died a little every day."

"I still love you, Laurie."

"How can you say that? You don't know what love is. If you loved me, how could you love what's her name?"

"Shari, and I don't love her. I love my son. He's a fine son, Laurie."

"If you loved me, you wouldn't have lived with her. You would have written to me and told me everything."

"I didn't know how to tell you... I felt so guilty."

"You could have come back and sent money or you could have brought him back with you."

"The authorities wouldn't let me have him because of my occupation...as for money, of course I will send it. Just a little goes a long way there."

"There's no use in talking about it. It's past, it's finished. I don't feel the same. I've been hurt too much."

"Do you mean that?"

"Yes."

She did not see him to the door when he left, but sat for a long time as if in a trance, stunned with hurt and loss. When she arose she noticed a small package on the coffee table and opened it. Inside was a string of real pearls. She had always wanted real pearls and here they were. They gave her no pleasure and she could never wear them. She remembered the small shell he had given her when they were children, that she still had among her keepsakes.

"Love is a trap," she said out loud, "nothing but a lousy trap."

She knew that, because Tom loved his son, he would want to see him… and Shari was, in some way, a threat. Tom was weak, and virile. How could she be at peace, knowing that every time he sailed to Tahiti he would be seeing Shari. It would never work. It could probably work for someone less sensitive, she thought, but not for me.

Laurie knew she should not see him again, for she would never feel good about herself if she did. But this was to prove the most difficult test of her will power that she was ever to experience.

He would phone her repeatedly, determined to break her resolve. When he told her that he loved her, that to be separated from her was torture, his voice felt like a caress, and when he finally did see her, his touch alone was enough to break her resolve. She tried seeing less of him, sometimes resisting for a few weeks to see if perhaps he would be easier to forget when she was absorbed in work and social activities.

But then something happened that made it easier to sever the ties because it was an emotionally traumatic experience. Tom showed up at a dance where he knew Laurie would be, with another woman on his arm. Desperate to regain her love, he thought a bit of jealousy might change her mind, but it had the opposite effect. Seeing the pity in her friend's eyes, Laurie felt humiliated, quickly left and somehow got home.

That night as she knelt before the fireplace, she destroyed in the flames every letter, every card, and anything Tom had ever given her, as she cried convulsively. While she was crying, the phone rang.

It was Douglas. Though he had kept in touch by letter now and then, he had never phoned her. She had been crying so hard that she could barely speak. He knew that Tom had come back because as friends they told each other everything.

To her surprise she heard his anger on the line as he said, "I had a very strong feeling that something was amiss. Get rid of the cad! I'm sure there are any number of men out there who would treat you in the manner you so richly deserve. Take my advice. It distresses me to think of you unhappy, especially when I am not able to help you."

It was the word cad that got to her. "Oh Douglas," she said, "you sound so sophisticated, even when you're angry and indignant." She laughed hysterically, as the tears streamed down her face.

That summer the Seaway dredging had pushed the waters from the shore of Riverside Drive and Laurie no longer had access to Moffatt's Island from St Lambert. It was with sadness that she made her last visit to the island. Her dad was feeling low as it was the last time he would fish in the river. He took her to the island by motor boat from Longueuil. She was to spend the day there and he would pick her up in the evening.

She was startled to find Tom there. He had been concealed behind some large boulders. "It was the only way I could see you," he said.

"How did you get here?"

He pointed to a canoe. "I paddled from port."

"But that's downstream, how will you get back? The current's too strong and it's far."

"I'll cut across to St Helen's Island or farther down if I have to, near Victoria Bridge."

"But you can't do that, it's rocky and dangerous! Nobody does it, not from here."

He laughed in his carefree way. "Nag me," he said "please nag me." A few strides and he had grabbed her by the arm and pulled her against him. "I need you Laurie," he whispered.

If he had not said those words, who knows, she might have succumbed, but she believed his love had deteriorated to a mere wanting, a basic lust. Her heart, still so naive, needed to hear different words. Nobody had ever told her that they loved her more than life, or more than God, or that they could not imagine living without her. These were not easy words for a man to say. Tom kissed her but she remained impassive.

A startled and disbelieving look crossed his face. "You must feel something, Laurie," he said softly.

"Yes, I feel sorry for you, you're pitiful."

She could tell by his face that he knew he had lost. He gathered up his things to leave. Laurie said, "You had better wait till my dad comes back. He'll show you the safest route; he knows the river like the back of his hand. He can take you to St Helen's by motor."

"I don't need anyone's help. I'm a fisherman and a sailor."

He cast off and she watched anxiously as he paddled. He headed directly across towards St Helen's. She knew that if he could make it there, he could portage around the island and then paddle to Montreal without difficulty. But the current mercilessly worked against him, forcing him to continue diagonally across to Victoria Pier, a much longer route, downstream. He was strong but he was not familiar with the place. There were hidden boulders everywhere under water.

Laurie remembered Tom's words. "Whenever we docked at some new port and I was warned not to go to a certain place because it was dangerous, well *that's* where I went." Danger attracted Tom; he was foolhardy.

She couldn't relax, but shaded her eyes and kept him in her sights. For some reason she recalled how once she believed that everyone had a Guardian Angel who helped them overcome danger. Sometimes she still believed it, possibly because she had children. She smiled ruefully thinking that Tom's Angel must surely be overworked, and because she felt frightened and helpless to do anything else, she prayed to her own Angel asking for assistance.

Just as she thought Tom was out of danger, the paddle was knocked from his hands and he lost control of the canoe. The current swiftly pulled him towards the rapids.

"Help him! help him!" she screamed, over and over again to all the powers that be, but as her voice was ripped from her throat by the wind, the canoe overturned and he was thrown into the water. He was a strong swimmer but he didn't have a chance.

Even when she no longer saw his golden hair, incoherently, crazily, and childishly, she continued to pray. Then she sank upon her knees and whispered, "I will always love you, Tommy Doyle."

21

It was a year later in the Fall when Douglas phoned to say that he had been transferred back to Ottawa. Although she missed him and wanted to see him, it was with an ambivalence that she went to meet him at the Dorval Airport.

She had endured more than enough of the emotional turmoil that seemed to be a part of loving. Many times she thought that it just wasn't worth it, until she remembered how it was when Tom and she had made love on the island. That was the way God had intended it to be between a man and a woman, she thought. Some people never experienced it at all, many because they are afraid to pay the price. She liked Douglas. He was the closest friend she had ever had, but if they should love each other would this change?

When she saw him coming through the exit, at first she didn't recognize him. It had only been two years, but he looked different, leaner and minus a moustache. This altered his appearance so dramatically that he gently brushed her memory of something forgotten.

Overjoyed to see her, he tried to hide it behind his natural reserve and perfect composure, but his eyes gave him away as usual.

"Welcome to Canada, old chap," Laurie said. She gave him a hug that put him off his guard, flustering him.

"Really Laurie! show some decorum in public," he said and then they both laughed. Those were the words he had used often when she did something completely un-British.

They drove to North Hatley for she wanted him to see Lake Massawippi in all of its Autumn splendour. "You have to travel far now," Laurie said, "to see the best that nature has to offer; it's not the same anymore."

They ate at a small country inn run by a Unitarian couple who were kindred spirits. The Unitarians, like their predecessors, the Quakers, believe that revelation can flow through anyone. They never place an obstacle between a man and his God.

Towards the end of the meal Douglas took Laurie's hand in his. He struggled with words.

"You're the first woman I have ever known, who made me think of marriage and now I am finally in the position to offer you something."

He fumbled on, but before he could go any further, Laurie enclosed his hand with both of hers and said, "You're the dearest friend I have ever had, but you deserve someone who can give you a lot more than I can."

He looked at her then with those eyes that made her want to give him her heart on a platter as he said, "Whatever am I going to do with the diamond?" He slowly opened a small piece of white paper. Inside rested a large diamond, and when he lowered his head, a tear fell upon it, causing a beam of light to shimmer on the wet stone. "I'm not very good with words, Laurie," he said, "but I had hoped."

A chill went down her spine, and then a sweet warmth enveloped her as it had in the dream nearly four years ago.

She spoke. "I'll be very proud to be your wife, Douglas, and as for the words, they have all been said."

Still Waters

That which I may give to you, though only in part,
comes from within where all is holy ground,
and the pulsing echo of my heart
sings silently of love, a secret sound.
There are songs of joy in this silence
that may never rise to speech,
but hover in smiles and then vanish.
Yet surely to God must they reach,
for I believe that God is Love,
and that His song will set me free,
and as near to Heaven on earth, my love,
as I can ever hope to be.

Epilogue

Moffatt's Island is no more. First access was cut off because of the Seaway, and then it was used as landfill to accommodate Expo '67. I remember when ice floes the size of cabins came down the river in the Spring with a roar and a display of grandeur so magnificent that you understood what the power of God meant. Wild ducks fed in the reeds and cried their nostalgic song in the Autumn. We fished and swam in the river and the water was so clean near the island that we could drink it.

Now we have what some call a miracle of engineering which means nothing to me, for how could it possibly compare to what was there before, that which lifted up our hearts and gave us a taste for Heaven.

Sources Consulted

The Canso Historical Society, Canso, Nova Scotia. 1963.

Dictionary of Canadian Biography, "George Moffatt," pages 553-556.

St Lambert, "The prairie called 'Mouille-Pie,'" Norma Stanley

Harding Moffatt — obituary, 1990.